To the Cleveland family

God bless you!

Viola Settles

MW01106026

This book plants a seed of hope in a world of painful circumstances.
—Renee Rowe, licensed therapist and owner of
Treeside Psychological Clinic

Linda has written a book that I would gladly offer to those with whom I visit in the hospital as well as to those in the church who seek to understand Biblical truths. —Chaplin and Methodist Minister Rose Poag, St. Joseph's Hospital, Hot Springs, Arkansas

Linda worked with me on some tough counseling assignments, applying the same kind of wisdom and insight into the struggles and triumphs of life that she demonstrates in her books. —Wesley Peterson, Pastor Emeritus, Christ the King Church, Oxford, Michigan

...insightful and interesting. —Theresa Hesch, counselor

When's the next one coming out? —Amber (ten years old)

I really liked it but there should be more blood and battles.
—Tyler (fifteen years old)

This book reminds me of the Chronicles of Narnia.
—Andrea (seventeen years old)

I want all my friends to read this book. —Bethany (sixteen years old)

Quest
for the
Other Kingdom

THE FIRST BOOK OF JOURNEYS

Quest
for the
Other Kingdom

THE FIRST BOOK OF JOURNEYS

by
Linda Settles

Edict House Publishing Group, LLC
Rustburg, Virginia

Quest for the Other Kingdom: The First Book of Journeys
© 2008 by Linda Settles

Edict House Publishing Group, LLC
Post Office Box 1304
Rustburg, VA 24588
Phone: 434-821-4005
www.EdictHouse.com
E-mail: EdictHouse@hotmail.com

Edict House books are available for special promotions, premiums and bulk discounts.

Editing by Dr. James R. Coggins, www.coggins.ca
Cover and interior design by Elizabeth Petersen
Book production by Cypress House
Cover and interior illustrations by Steve Ferchaud

Publisher's Cataloging-in-Publication Data

Settles, Linda.
    The first book of journeys / Linda Settles. — 1st ed. — Rustburg, VA :
Edict House, 2008.
    p. ; cm.
    (Quest for the other kingdom ; 1)
    ISBN: 978-0-9790238-0-4
    Audience: 4th grade.

Summary: A young slave named Brae dares to follow the Messenger and flee the service of Meriquoi, searching for the Other Kingdom across the sea, ruled with justice and mercy by the great King Immon. Will he survive the dangerous journey? Or perish on the Sea of Life?

    1. Fantasy fiction, American—Juvenile literature. 2. [Fantasy.]
I. Title. II. Series.
    PZ7.S5123 F57   2008 2007940749
    [E]—dc22 0804

Printed in the United States of America
2 4 6 8 9 7 5 3 1
First edition

Dedicated to my husband Michael
You are my beacon in the storms that arise
on the Sea of Life.

And to my daughters
Christina, scholar and friend, and
Bethany, joyful socialite and shopping buddy.

Table of Contents

Acknowledgements

To Cynthia Frank, my mentor. You have taught me so much about the world of books and have become a friend in the process.

To my editor, Dr. James R. Coggins. Your insight and encouragement as well as your relentless insistence on clarity and accuracy have contributed much to the development of this book.

To Eve Warnez, the first fellow-writer to critique my story and return it with red markings. Thanks, Eve, for preparing my fragile psyche for the pen and ink of professional editors.

To all my friends and colleagues who have read my manuscript and given me great feedback.

To my nieces and nephews who gave me rave reviews.

Introduction

T he City of Bondage is ancient, nearly as old as the earth on which it stands. Gentle breezes ruffle the fronds that umbrella from the tops of fruited palms. Standing like silent sentries, they cast thin shadows upon the shore, where restless waves claw the golden sand.

Shade is rare in the city, and reserved primarily for the comfort of the high and mighty, the rich and influential. Copper benches, adorned with rosettes and miniature fluted columns, grace the shade beneath cocoa palms and building overhangs.

Slaves and other minor subjects of the city find some small relief from the searing rays of the tropical sun by lingering in the shelter of ramshackle kiosks on dusty lanes.

Their funds exhausted, the newly arrived are forced to serve wealthy merchants in exchange for daily bread. Others have been torn from their native homes by those who trade in human flesh. A favored few are born into the city and embrace a citizenship that affords them wealth and prestige, a heritage that ensures unquestioning allegiance to Dagog, supreme ruler over the city.

CHAPTER 1

The Journey Begins

N o one noticed the freckle-faced youth who stood beside the merchant's table, peering over piles of pottery and bright bolts of cloth. Brae's straw-colored hair seemed to have a mind of its own, sticking up like fresh-tossed hay in every direction. His green eyes squinted into the glare of the noonday sun.

"Where is the Messenger?" Brae was growing impatient. He had been told that the Messenger, emissary of the great King Immon, would come to the City of Bondage with the power to free the slaves of Meriquoi. Every day in the kiosk, Brae watched and waited as he counted change and wrapped the purchases of Meriquoi's customers. Every beating he endured beneath Meriquoi's whip, every kick from his polished boot, made him long for the Messenger's arrival.

Brae scanned the ragged tops of cocoa palms etched against a cloudless sky, seeking the feathered friend that kept him distant company as he hawked his master's wares. Brae could not remember when he had first seen the bird. It had always been there. Thinking that the white bird might not show today, he finished serving his customer. From the shadows of the kiosk, he watched the dusty crowd as it wound through the congested marketplace.

The crowd parted, flowing away from a man who stood a head taller than those around him. The man exuded confidence, from his silver-gray hair to the tip of his leather boots. His golden-brown eyes seemed quick and alert beneath neatly trimmed brows. His tanned face revealed smile lines at the corner of his mouth above a firm jaw. His tunic, blazing crimson in the morning light, attested his nobility.

Curious stares turned toward the stranger and then downward. Most of the citizens of the city seemed reluctant to meet his direct gaze. He paid them no heed as his long strides carried him swiftly toward the kiosk where Brae stood partially hidden behind bolts of cloth stacked high on the table.

Could this be the Messenger? Brae wondered and felt his palms grow sweaty.

Disdaining the glances of the unruly crowd, the stranger moved easily along the road, his eyes wide, scanning the kiosks that lined the dusty avenue.

He is searching for me! Brae thought, his heart racing. Stepping out of the shadows, he stared boldly at the stranger. The Messenger nodded at Brae and moved on, small puffs of dust rising with each footfall. Brae slipped away from the kiosk and blended into the crowd, following a few feet behind the stranger. Brae's breath came in short gasps as he raced to keep up with the long paces of the Messenger.

With a start, Brae realized they had turned a corner and were heading toward the shipyard. "By the gods…" Brae stopped abruptly and took a step backward. "Does he expect me to become a stowaway?"

I know what will happen to me if I am caught, he thought, and misery clutched at his throat like an iron fist.

Brae tried not to think of other slaves who had attempted escape. Meriquoi knew well how to make an example of anyone who dared defy him. His skill with the whip was well known in the City of Bondage; he could flay the flesh from a slave's back and put him back to work a day later.

"I will probably be reassigned to Jamie's job," Brae fretted. His misery escalated as he imagined himself carrying the sloppy chamber pots across the polished floors of Meriquoi's elegant house.

Stuffing his fists into the pockets of his tattered, ankle-length pants, Brae kept walking, barely aware of the burning sand on his bare feet.

Turning, the Messenger beckoned the boy to follow him across a short, narrow bridge onto the deck of a small ship. It bore the name *Seeking*. The sun glistened on the varnished mahogany decking. Weathered masts reached for the clouds above the emerald waters of the bay. The ship, rocking in the gentle swells, seemed friendly somehow.

Before his fear could force him to return to the momentary safety of the kiosk, Brae stepped onto the deck and looked around. "Where am I to hide?"

The Messenger seemed surprised. "You do not hide aboard the good ship *Seeking*, my son." He paused, and then a smile broke across his face, like the bright lip of the sun breaking above gray clouds. "You are under the protection of the great King Immon."

"Immon..." Brae rolled the name slowly off his tongue. "King of the Other Kingdom?" Brae knew that he parroted the words of Belita, but he had little knowledge of the great king other than what the Teller of Stories had imparted to him.

"Yes. This ship is in his service. If you depart these shores in the *Seeking*, you declare that you seek a country whose founder and royal governor is the great King Immon."

"But what if this King Immon will not allow me to enter his country?"

The Messenger nodded, conceding his point. "You are not yet ready to live in the Other Kingdom, Brae, for doubt rules in your heart. But the journey on the Sea of Life is long, and you will have opportunity to decide what you will do before you meet the great king.

Brae stared hard at the Messenger. Something about him reminded the boy of Belita, the Teller of Stories, who had entered the house of Meriquoi when Brae was a child of six summers. Patting the place on the rough plank floors before the stone fireplace in the slave quarters, she had smiled at Brae, and he had crept like an abandoned puppy, wary of kindness, to her side. He had leaned against her and listened to her stories night after night. She told of the great King Immon and of his father, the Emperor Addar, Supreme Ruler of Kingdoms. "Addar is a mighty warrior," she had said, "yet he is as gentle as a lamb with his own children, especially his beloved son Immon." She had spoken tenderly, almost as if speaking of her own son, weaving a verbal tapestry of love and suffering, joy and anguish that seemed too good to be true.

The Messenger looked away from Brae, a grim expression, like the darkening clouds of an imminent storm, crossing his face. "The Kingdom awaits you, Brae, but there is not time for delay. Will you go or do you choose to stay?"

Brae followed the Messenger's gaze, and terror, like the breaking of an angry sea, washed over him, for a cloud of dust rose from the pounding of feet along the road as twenty angry men raced toward the bay. Leading the pack was Meriquoi—saber in hand, wild eyes glazed, crooked teeth bared, like a tiger bereft of its prey.

There was no turning back. Brae nodded to the Messenger. "Yes. I will go."

The Messenger loosed the mooring ropes and began unfurling the sails, motioning to Brae to take the wooden wheel and guide the ship out of the bay.

Brae stared at the mob swarming toward the ship. Terror glued his feet to the planked deck, his throat tightened into a twisted knot, and his knees began to buckle as the angry men drew near.

"Brae!" the Messenger spoke sharply.

Brae leapt into action. He grabbed the wheel, feeling the ship glide away from the dock. The sails unfurled, instantly catching the sudden gust of wind that sprang out of nowhere—pushing the *Seeking* beyond the reach of Meriquoi.

The dark face of Brae's former master was crimson in his rage and scrunched like a sun-dried prune as he stood, half squatting in fury. His heavy lips mouthed words that Brae could easily imagine. Brae was glad he could not hear the profanities as the stretch of water widened between the ship and those who paced the dock shaking their fists toward heaven.

The wheel of the *Seeking* felt strange in Brae's hands. He stared at them: browned by the sun and callused by hard work. He wondered that they held the helm of a ship, wondered that he had dared defy his master, certain that death would be the price of his defiance.

The sea, foaming above the gentle swells, stretched as far as the eye could see to meet the salty blue horizon. The *Seeking* slipped over a swell and dipped into a trough, rising quickly to catch the ridge of another swell and point its prow toward the sun riding high in the sky. In his anxiety, Brae imagined the *Seeking* was a great bird whose pinions spread across the waters to carry him into grave danger on uncharted seas.

Brae stared hard at the man who leaned on the starboard rail, just a few feet from where he stood torn by doubt. Brae spat the bitterness from his mouth. Life in the City of Bondage was hard, but Brae wondered if he had traded a familiar misery for a worse one.

What have I done? he worried, as the City of Bondage faded in the distance. *I don't know this man. What if he is a slaver, or worse, one of the Mystics from the deep, wrapped in the flesh of man?*

Brae's knuckles whitened and he leaned on the wheel for support. He had often dreamt of Mystics and their ghostly ships during the past nine years, for nine years it was since he had boarded the strange craft that sailed into the harbor of the City of Bondage late one night under the cover of a thousand thunderheads.

The black ship, riding heavy in the water, was strangely dark. The few candles that flickered about the deck illuminated faces that seemed somehow... inhuman. Guttural sounds, like the voices of the damned, escaped the hold and among the unfamiliar words Brae thought he heard "help" and "lost."

This ship, Brae thought, *reeks of death.* Then he saw the flagstaff atop the towering mast and forgot to breathe.

A fierce beast, neither bird nor reptile, belched fire and smoke among the troubled clouds, and blood ran red, flowing down the fluttering rag and dripping, or so it seemed, along the mast to spill upon the beams below.

It is not real, the boy thought, repeating the phrase in his head until it became a chant, though not a word squeaked past his lips. *It is a flag, nothing more.*

He would never forget his master's face that night. Eyes fevered with excitement, bulbous nose flaring in the candlelight as he nudged young Brae along, mop and bucket in hand, and made him join a dozen other slaves already on their knees amid the filthy suds that sloshed about the deck.

Sailors in tattered clothing, long soiled by the journey of a thousand nautical miles and some quest known only to themselves and Meriquoi, stalked the deck. A bag of money changed hands and Brae was certain he had been sold along with the others to the captain of the dark ship. He trembled so violently that one of the crew noticed his tremors. Laughter roared and a kick to the seat of his pants sent Brae sprawling on his belly on the slick deck.

"What? You don't care to join our party?" The captain grasped Brae's shirt and pulled him close, expelling his sour breath into the boy's face. Brae longed to close his eyes, blot out the sneering face, the yellowed teeth.

"Let me tell you a story, boy," the captain said, and settled himself on a barrel near the rail. "Take a seat." He shoved Brae toward a crate at his feet. Other sailors gathered around, sipping from brown bottles and leering in Brae's direction.

"There's things out on that mother-sea," the captain began, "that a little boy like you don't even want to know about. We seen 'em…." He paused as if waiting for agreement from his crew.

"Sure we seen 'em," an emaciated sailor said, scratching at his neck with dirt-encrusted nails.

"They ain't like nothin' you ever seen," said another.

Brae knew that his eyes had dilated and his heart pounded visibly in his chest. There was no twinkle in the sailors' eyes; they meant every word of it.

"Now, there's a lot of ornery beasts lives out there in that mother-sea," the captain continued, resting his back against the rail, "but there ain't none worse than the wist. A Mystic of the foulest order. Alive they were, once, and then dead. And now they's both dead and alive and lookin' for meat. They comes to devour little boys like you, so don't you ever take to sea, 'cause when you do, you gonna meet em' and you ain't never gonna get out alive."

It was dead silent on that secret ship except for the furled sails flapping on the yards. Brae wanted to look away from the captain's eyes but could not seem to do it. Suddenly, thunder roared and lightning crashed through the sky. It struck the metal rail and sizzled like rain on hot stones. It took Brae a moment to realize that the captain was no longer sitting, but lay flat on the deck, his mouth agape, his dead eyes staring at the low black clouds hanging over the mast.

Brae felt a hand dig into his shoulder and looked up into the bulging eyes of his master. "Let's go, boy," Meriquoi said. Brae stumbled to his feet and blindly followed his master, eyes squeezed shut in the face of death.

Belita had found him scrunched into a corner beside his cot, eyes wide. "A dream, young Brae?" she had asked. He opened his mouth to speak but words failed him.

Belita took his hand and led him to the kitchen. Wrapping him in a warm blanket, she made tea and sat across from him at the massive oak table.

The light of dawn was creeping through the window above the table when Belita put an arm around his shoulders and walked him back to his bed.

∾

A thousand nightmares later, Brae stood at the wheel of the *Seeking*, unable to forget. His stomach felt on fire, as if a cauldron of fear boiled inside him. *I am not ready for this*, he thought, but did not say it. The *Seeking* sped on the wings of the wind toward a destination unknown to the boy, who stood with his gaze fastened on his deliverer.

Brae studied the face of the man who promised him freedom. This stranger was asking Brae to trust him. Trust did not come easily to one raised in the house of Meriquoi, where deception was prized above integrity and cunning above valor.

The golden-brown eyes that stared into Brae's were confident, mysterious. *Almost*, Brae thought, *like Belita's eyes.* Memories sprang unbidden to the slave boy's mind and he looked away, unwilling to yield to the hot tears that always accompanied memories of Belita. After a moment in which time stood still, Brae once again sought the eyes of the Messenger and found himself staring into pools of memory, swimming in the waters of the past. He yielded to the flow, allowing himself to remember Belita's laughter, warm with affection; the kind hand that ruffled his hair as he sat before the dying embers of the evening fires, already dreading the cold that would creep into his bones when he climbed the narrow stairway to the attic cubbyhole that he called home.

By night he had listened to her stories, by day he had endured the pain, the humiliation, and the threats of Meriquoi; and what he had believed in the night seemed but the fancies of an old woman in the light of day. And so he vacillated between hope and despair, between invisible truths and daily disappointments that threatened to drag him into the muck of resignation, committing him forever to slavery in the City of Bondage.

Not all the slaves of Meriquoi had been pleased when Belita spoke of the Messenger. Some were angry, displeased that anyone should challenge their complacency.

"I will believe it when I see it!" a thin youth had muttered, fists clenched at his sides. His back was crisscrossed with the scars of many beatings.

"No, my son," Belita had said. "You will see it when you can believe it."

At first Brae too thought Belita spoke the foolishness of an old woman, one who dreamt too much. But she was so confident, so certain that Immon would send his Messenger to those who called out to him—those who refused to be silenced—that Brae dared hope, maybe even believe, that life existed somewhere beyond the City of Bondage, that somehow, someday, he could be free. When he began to doubt, Belita always knew. She would chide, "Do not fear, young Brae. One day—you will see!"

How strong she was. *But not strong enough.* Once again Brae's eyes filled with tears and he blinked, ashamed to cry in the presence of the stranger who stood beside him, watching, waiting, somehow *knowing*, it seemed, that even though he stood aboard the *Seeking* he was not yet committed to the journey.

"There is one thing that you must know," the Messenger's face became solemn. "Immon has an enemy. He is called Dagog, Prince of the Darkness. He is lord over the evil master whom you have served from your birth, and lord over all the Kingdom of Adawm. If you leave these shores, he will do all that is in his power to destroy you."

"But he cannot… right?" Brae asked hopefully. "I mean, if I am under the protection of Immon—"

"Immon promises you life in the Other Kingdom, Brae. He does not say that you will not suffer. For it is impossible for anyone to enter into that fair land without having suffered in this one."

Returning the Messenger's firm gaze, Brae felt his doubt and fears melt away like butter beneath the burning rays of the sun. Resolve hardened his words. "I would rather die trying to escape than live any longer in the City of Bondage."

Brae felt older than his seventeen years as he leaned into the wind. He glanced back at the city. It was the only home he had ever known. Home. He shrugged. *There is no home for a slave.*

Brae turned away from the City of Bondage, determined that he would never again look back. As he did so, a dark shadow passed over the *Seeking*. Brae gasped and peered into the clouds. There was nothing in the sky but pale blue space, white clouds, and a couple of seagulls. Nothing more.

"It is Dagog, Prince of the Darkness." The Messenger was grim.

At these words, Brae became aware of the smell of sulfur. The sea seemed shrouded in a strange gray mist, though the sun blazed upon the water as brightly as before. Brae wondered whether the mist was real or only a figment of his imagination.

At the sound of huge wings flapping lazily against the currents of the sky, Brae's courage failed; he looked at the water, measuring the distance to shore. The angry mob had dispersed. *No one would notice if I slipped back into the city, he thought. Perhaps I could change my appearance, assume a different name. I could find a place on one of the islands near the city, where I could work for the fishermen. They always need boys to mend their nets, scrub their boats.*

A squat, powerful figure returned to the dock, right hand on his sheathed saber and his left shielding his eyes from the glare as he stared across the deep blue waters of the bay. *Even if the man on the dock is Meriquoi,* Brae reasoned, *there is no way he can reach across the waves to capture me.* Such logic did little to lessen the terror that threatened to emasculate the runaway slave.

The Messenger was silent. A seagull chattered overhead. Waves slapped at the sides of the ship. The hot sun shimmered on the water. Brae turned to look across the open water that stretched to infinity before him and noted the draconic shadow that draped itself across the waves, rising and falling on the cresting seas. Dagog, it seemed, would stalk him to the ends of the earth.

Brae clenched the wheel with both hands and faced the horizon, glad that the Messenger was at his side as he fled the City of Bondage and began his journey on the Sea of Life.

CHAPTER 2

The Ancient Book of Mysteries

B rae studied the ancient manuscripts, charts, and maps in the captain's quarters. He was intrigued by one especially large volume called the *Ancient Book of Mysteries*. The front of the brown leather book was adorned with the picture of a silver birch tree. A thick trunk, somewhat gnarled by time and perhaps by the abuse of battles fought beneath its silvered canopy, occupied the center of the cover.

Belita had loved "the Tree." Her voice had always dropped in pitch and grown soft when she spoke of it. Brae had felt as he had when watching a tender love scene in one of the many dramas presented for all to see on the streets of the City of Bondage. Even in that city, the love of a man for a maiden was sometimes portrayed as a pure and beautiful mystery.

Late one evening, Brae opened the *Ancient Book* and sat on his bed. With the thick volume propped on his lap, he began to read. The letters were strange to him, though beautiful, with graceful curves and flowing endings that made him feel as if he were entering the private world of an author whose scholarship and authority marked him a great and noble dignitary. Embarrassed and somewhat intimidated by his intrusion into what he now perceived to be a collection of private letters by this unknown person, Brae felt he should close the book. But he found it impossible to do so.

The candle burned low as Brae turned the pages. The words meant little to him, as their meaning seemed far beyond his understanding. But the illustrations, they were a different matter.

There were pictures of battles fought by men with swords and armor. Sometimes they fought against human foes and the blood ran thick and red. In other pictures, they fought against creatures so grotesque and horrible that Brae quickly turned the pages.

At some point, Brae realized with a start that the candle had burned out. The pages of the *Ancient Book* were illuminated by a soft golden glow from within. Brae closed the book and backed away from the bed, afraid now to touch the strange volume.

He pulled his blanket off the end of the bed and wrapped himself in it on the floor. The gentle roll of the *Seeking* and the soft moaning of the wind through the rigging comforted him, as a child rocked in his mother's arms. He fell into the embrace of the night with a deep sigh as loneliness paid him an unexpected visit. He longed for something, or someone, but did not know what or whom. A longing he could not understand became an ache in his heart as hunger pains the belly when one has been long deprived of food.

The stars grew dim in the night sky as the morning light supplanted the darkness. Still Brae slept, dreaming of battles and monsters and strange lights that illuminated his room and penetrated his flesh. Condensing finally somewhere inside him, a soothing presence cooled the heat of his loneliness and filled the cavernous void in a chamber in which a single piece of furniture rocked back and forth.

In the days that followed, Brae thought often of the *Ancient Book*. He had returned it to its place on the mahogany desk that occupied a corner of his room. Sometimes, on the darkest of nights, he would awaken and notice that the silver birch tree glowed softly in the darkness. Brae felt compelled to open the book and allow himself to be drawn into its pages, to become a part of the history written there; but at the same time repelled by the sacrifice that he intuitively understood such a decision would require of him. Brae had fled the tyranny of Meriquoi but he had taken the City of Bondage with him in his heart.

The Messenger was not deceived. "You have to let it go," he said one day as they sat at the table in the galley.

"What?" Brae asked, startled. In his mind, Brae had wandered down the shadowed lanes of the City of Bondage. On the screen of his memory he watched scenes of horror and tantalizing frenzy as men and women fed upon the lust that fueled the city and acted out fantasies of outrage against their fellow men. Feeling guilty, but also amazed at the Messenger's uncanny ability to discern his thoughts, Brae became angry. "I don't know what you're talking about!" he said.

The Messenger stood and walked up the steps to the rail. A brisk wind billowed the sails of the *Seeking*. Brae followed the Messenger up the stairs to the bridge and took the wheel. Roiling black clouds hung low over the horizon and rain began to pelt the rising waves. Night came early without stars or moon. The *Seeking* rose on the crest of each wave and crashed into the foaming troughs between.

Brae was glad of the rain, for it masked the tears that trailed down his face as he stood at the wheel alone in the dark and the storm.

CHAPTER 3

Doubt Breeds Despair

T he following day dawned clear and bright. The air smelled as fresh and clean as sun-dried laundry. Brae leaned against the rail, his eyes closed, remembering.

A little boy of about seven years, he had been assigned the task of helping Belita take care of Meriquoi's laundry. He took each fine cotton garment, still damp from the washing, out of the wicker basket and shook it out, handing it to Belita who fastened it to the wire line that stretched across a hidden alcove on Meriquoi's estate.

Once again, longing created an agonizing ache in Brae's chest as he remembered the tropical paradise of Meriquoi's gardens. He could smell the fruity fragrance of blood-red bromeliads with their evergreen fans, feel the shade of white bird of paradise with its dark green leaves and bright yellow fruit. Cool breezes swept across the enormous fountain centered with a bronze sculpture of the entwined bodies of a naked couple.

"Brae." The voice of the Messenger interrupted Brae's journey into the past, a place already changing in the young man's mind, metamorphosing into something that it was not—paradise without pain. "You need to remember the pain."

"Why?" Brae's face flushed with anger. "Why can't I just forget all that and keep the good memories?"

"Because it is the Truth that sets you free, Brae, and distorted truths are only lies masquerading as reality."

"So what if they're lies? If my lies make me happy, why should you care?"

"Because happiness built on lies is like a house of sticks built upon the embers of a dying fire. It may warm you at first, but in the end it will enflame your house and scatter your ashes in the wind. Get to know the Truth, Brae, for Truth alone can set you free."

Brae turned on his heel and stalked to his room. He threw himself on his bed, refusing to glance in the direction of the *Ancient Book of Mysteries*. The silver birch tree with its gentle illumination mocked him now.

Another storm broke upon the horizon and Brae climbed the steps to stand staring into the purple-gray darkness. An oddly shaped cloud, sharp beaked and ominous, stretched across the canvas of the sky. A lighter mist of dirty gray splayed across the space beyond it, and the smell of sulfur hung heavy on the wet, cold air.

Brae shivered. "It is just a cloud," he spoke aloud as he crossed the deck to take the wheel of the *Seeking*.

"Do you really think an Other Kingdom exists?" the throaty whisper coming from somewhere inside his head neither surprised nor intimidated

Brae; it seemed natural and somehow familiar.

Belita was certain that it did. Brae thought, remembering the faraway expression on her face when she spoke of the Other Kingdom, as if she could see through some invisible doorway into a different world. Brae blinked back tears, remembering the ship that had brought Belita to the shores of his city.

The *Scavenger* was owned by a ruthless merchant whose teeth were capped with gold, and his one eye squeezed into a perpetual squint. His other eye had been, so they said, pierced by the spear of an angry boy whose father lay squirming in the net of the slavers along with a dozen of his neighbors—ambushed at the village council and then herded like cattle into the bowels of the ship.

Some said that Belita was the wife of one of the men, that she clung to his arm and was dragged along with the others to the *Scavenger* and thrown into the hold.

She had stood on the slave block staring into the clouds, heavy and dark against the heavens. She had refused to watch as the men from her village, every one of them, were led away, bound by a common rope, and forced to board another ship, the *Scabbard*, bound for faraway lands.

Left alone, Belita shed no tears. She did not struggle as Meriquoi paid the slaver a meager price and laid a rough hand on her shoulder, pushing her along the dusty road to his house as if she were a thing that could be bought! *The more Meriquoi mistreated her,* Brae recalled, *the kinder she became, like a ripe fruit that became sweeter with the bruising.*

Though the drizzle continued, the sun came out from behind the clouds and beacons of light shone like golden cones upon the face of the sea.

Brae shook his head. *What is getting into me? I'm not even sure the Other*

Kingdom exists; and if it does, I'm not certain I want to go there. Resentment flooded over him like an angry wave.

Belita was my friend, but she was a slave, like me. If there is an Other Kingdom, and if the king of that Kingdom is a great and powerful ruler—Brae slammed his fist down on the wooden wheel—*then why did he let her die?*

This was abruptly followed by a guilty conscience as Brae conceded that *someone* had sent the Messenger in the *Seeking* to deliver him from the hands of Meriquoi. Still, Belita's kind, benevolent king seemed incongruent with the disinterested sovereign who would allow his faithful subject to be mutilated by the likes of Meriquoi.

During the days that followed, as Brae sailed through warm sunshine and cool cleansing rains, the buried sorrow of seventeen years of bondage rose to the surface as oil rises in water.

CHAPTER 4

The Assignment

D agog was at ease in his domain—the Middle Clouds—a dark and dangerous habitation forged in ancient times between the heavens and the earth. Invincible in its invisibility, it was subject only to those whose authority was feared and detested by the "powers of the air," as the emperor himself had titled the dragon and his followers.

The roiling black clouds, pierced occasionally by violent electrical spears, soothed him, for tempest and turmoil were his delight. Seated upon a mountain of smoky cloud, he crossed his legs and folded his wings at his sides. His students, the most elite class from the realm of the living dead, sat in a semicircle around him.

"I have an assignment for one of you," the beast began. "There has been… a deserter in the Kingdom of Adawm. A slave boy by the name of Brae has fled the shores of the City of Bondage." The expected sound of grinding teeth and sucked-in breath mingled with the rumble of thunder. "I have… concerns. Every deserter that leaves our ranks and aligns himself with the Dreadful One will win others to His side. Apparently, not all my students have learned the art of deception as well as you have."

At these words of flattery, the bowed heads of Dagog's subjects bent even lower until it appeared that they would snap right off their necks. Dagog smiled, not a pleasant sight, for there was no affection in it.

"Umbler!" He called upon a junior dragon—a form-changer like himself. "You are in charge of the deserter who travels aboard the *Seeking* with the… the…"

Dagog, as usual, had a hard time speaking the name of the Messenger. He hated him, but could not deny a certain admiration for one superior in every way to himself. His subjects understood and wisely decided to nod their agreement, ignoring this small weakness on the part of their master. "You must persuade him to forsake the journey on which he has embarked."

Umbler knelt before Dagog and received his charge. "Do not fail me!" Dagog thundered and the heavens cringed before his foul breath. He did not have to expand upon his threat, for all his subjects trembled, knowing already that Umbler was not truly fortunate to be chosen for this task. They, one and all, were secretly relieved that they had not received the honor.

Umbler asked, "Do I have your permission, oh Great Master, to use all means at my disposal to assure our success?"

"You must." Dagog answered, for he knew that along with the seeds of doubt sown into Brae's young heart by the subjects of Dagog, seeds of hope had been sown by the woman who loved him as her own son. He grimaced at this, consoled only by the memory of the punishment awarded the student who had failed to conquer the woman whose name was Belita. But that, of course, is another story, one that Dagog was not interested in thinking about.

The meeting adjourned, Umbler sailed the currents of the sky under the canopy of night. Scratching at the mottled wart that dangled from the right side of his nose, he plotted the destruction of one who had escaped the shores of the City of Bondage but had not yet surrendered his allegiance to the king of the Other Kingdom.

The irritated wart had begun to bleed. "This is the time to get him," Umbler exulted, enjoying the caress of darkness against his scaled body. Obsessed with his plans, he bumped into a star and fell through the sky, landing with a splash upon his bottom. He found it difficult to think for a few days due to the pounding ache in his head, so it took him awhile to make his first move.

CHAPTER 5

The Port of Plenty

D ays passed into weeks, and the supply of food and water aboard the *Seeking* dwindled. The wind, howling over the Sea of Life, grew cold and sharp, nipping at Brae's exposed elbows and legs. Shoulders hunched against the wind, Brae shivered in his rags, his tattered shirt and the thin fabric of his short pants affording little protection from the weather. He was huddled in a corner, wishing for his old room in the attic in the City of Bondage, when he saw smoke rising into the white clouds. He scrambled to the rail and saw that the *Seeking* was approaching land. A wooden sign anchored in the sand bore the words PORT OF PLENTY.

The Messenger laid a hand on Brae's arm. "Do not forget that you are in search of the Other Kingdom." His kind eyes looked concerned. "You will find danger even in the Port of Plenty."

As the Messenger began furling the sails, Brae prepared to drop anchor. When the ship had drifted into the shelter of the harbor, Brae launched a small boat and rowed hard toward the port, his eyes fixed upon the shore. Had he looked up, he would have seen the winged monster that glided through the white fleece of clouds above his head. Had he seen the crimson streak that trailed behind the creature, bleeding into a pink-tinged column and then dissipating in the faint blush of the setting sun, Brae would have spun the small craft and headed back to the *Seeking* as fast as he could row. Had he looked to the starboard side of his craft and seen the dark reptilian shadow on the water, he might have been spared the sorrows that would soon befall him.

The Messenger, whose sharp eyes watched from the rail of the *Seeking,* squinted into the wounded sky. He grieved for the boy who approached the shoreline of the Port of Plenty, ignorant of the injury that might befall one who accepts such bounty without recognizing the source of his provision.

A few children played in the sand beneath the weathered sign that bore the name of the village. They shouted when they saw Brae. Men and women came running, their faces wreathed in smiles, their voices excited. "Welcome!" they said over and over.

Brae smiled back, holding out his hands to the children, who grabbed him and pulled him toward a great fire in the village square. The villagers prepared a feast, piling a wooden table high with fresh meat and steaming corn, potatoes, and fried cakes dipped in honey. As the sun slipped beneath the flaming waters of the sea, Brae, his stomach full, strolled over to the fire to sit cross-legged beside a muscular young man whom he later learned was the son of Anthar, governor of the Port of Plenty. He warmed his back at the fire, content to sit there, listening to the chatter of the women, the blustering of the young men, and the squealing laughter of children.

The night grew cold, and mothers carried their children off to bed. A few old men told outrageous tales of visitors who had come to the Port of Plenty in times past.

A toothless crone with stick-thin legs and gray hair knotted at the nape of her wrinkled neck listened as if paying little attention to the ramblings of men who had outlived their purpose and now spent their days reinventing the past.

A full moon high overhead silvered the sandy shore and the lush palms that bordered the city. Brae glanced at the good ship *Seeking* bobbing on the gentle swells in the harbor.

There is a certain... mystery about the old ship, he thought. A twinge of longing stirred somewhere deep inside him, so far down beneath the joy of unfamiliar pleasures that Brae hardly noticed it. Then it passed, and he was glad to have his feet planted on the good earth. His eyes began to droop, and the droning voices had grown dim, when something startled him wide-awake.

It was the old woman, speaking in a singsong voice.

> There's others that's come this way before
> To mend their boats and refill their stores.
> They gave us more than they took from us
> And the King of the Kingdom of Adawm it was

That sent them here and gave us the heart
To fill up their boats and to do our part
To get them along on their merry way
To the Other Kingdom without delay.
But to those that come to take our best
With their own uncaring selfishness
A curse I say! A double one too,
And if you don't like it—a curse on you!
There's foul afoot: I seen the beast
Flying high in the sky when we was at feast.
Happy he's not, trouble is sure.
He's heading, I think, for the Valley of E'ure.
Where once a time, yes, long ago,
He was beat at his game, but doesn't know.
So after this boy, I am sure that he is,
For the King has called, but it is not yet His.
Safe it is not, this boy from the ship,
For the Folk in the Port are no matter to it
Sleeping away the last of the night.
If you listen to me you will send it aflight.
Trouble will come an' I say it ain't long
For this boy—it ain't no friend of Immon.

Brae opened one eye a tiny bit, hoping his long lashes would conceal the fact that he was not sleeping. Then he saw her. The crone was swaying back and forth as if to inaudible music, chanting the words through wrinkled lips, eyes wide, unblinking, like the eyes a cadaver. Her thin fingers raked the air, her long black talons curving around a hidden object known only to herself. She reached out her bony arms and drew them back in a swimming motion. She was still caught up in her private drama when the old men got up, one by one, shaking their heads and turned from the fire to retire, each to his own house.

Alone with the old woman, Brae found it impossible to keep up the pretense of sleep, so he sat up, rubbing his eyes as if just awakened.

"Humph!" she said, getting to her feet and abruptly turning her back on him. She walked away without a word and Brae sat trembling before the dying fire, glad that the night was almost over.

Within minutes, dawn broke across the horizon and the sky burst into flames of gold and crimson. Dew-drenched palms glistened black against the breaking day, changing slowly in the brightening sun to shades of gray. Their verdant foliage swept the sky like lazy fingers in the morning breeze. Dogs barked. The village was waking.

CHAPTER 6

A Journey Forsaken

After breakfast Anthar sent his servant to lead Brae to a house at the edge of the village. Surrounded by lazy palms and pink bromeliads, the lawn stretched to the white sands that met the emerald sea. Brae's breath caught in his throat. *Does this mean that I am to live here?* he thought, amazed at his good fortune.

Two women, hardly older than he, stood in the doorway like children eager for approval. Brae entered, looked around at the clean, well-appointed dwelling, and nodded his thanks. One of the women handed him a stack of soft woolen blankets and a strange object the like of which he had never seen.

"What is this?" He held up the long stick, which had bristles, like the hair of a wild boar, fastened in the end.

The women looked at each other and giggled. One of them took it from his hand and began to brush her hair with it. Handing it back to him, she stepped outside, stifling a laugh until she and her companion were out of sight.

Brae crossed the room to sit on the bed. Filled with goose down, it was as soft as a pillow. Bright rugs adorned the planed wooden floor. The fragrance of orchids permeated the room. *If only Belita could see me now*, Brae thought, his chest swelling with pride. *How do you like this, Meriquoi?* He grinned.

Autumn yielded to winter, and winter to spring. Still Brae lingered in the Port of Plenty. He no longer looked toward the sea. He tried to forget that the Messenger waited aboard the *Seeking*. He refused to think of the Messenger's warning. He could see no danger here. The Messenger could go on waiting.

Brae spent most of the day lying in the hammock that swung between two palms and playing with the children in the sand. He chose to ignore the disdain of the young men who glanced his way as they did their work, the women talking behind their hands. He looked away from the baleful stares of Anthar's eldest son, Jiron, whose house now belonged to Brae. *Governor Anthar remains friendly*, Brae thought, *so why should I care?*

One summer day when the sun shimmered on the waves and the rhythm of the surf lulled even the most active child into the shade for a nap, Brae lay in the hammock, dimly aware of a shadow, long and dark, that passed between the sun and his closed eyes.

He tried not to think of it, yet in the weeks that followed, he dreamt often of a sprawling shadow floating in grotesque distortions over swelling waves, accompanied always by the acidic odor of sulfur that stung his nostrils. The smell lingered long after sleep had fled and left Brae trembling in the darkness.

One night, Brae was roused from peaceful slumber by the vague sorts of sounds that often disturb one's sleep without fully rousing one. There was a quarter moon that night and few stars, rendering the darkness thick and black. The sound of feet pounding along the dirt path outside his door aroused Brae further, just in time to see shadowy forms disappear into the forest, bundles of his belongings spilling from their hands.

Something fell in the house, making a loud noise against the floor. Fully awake now, Brae saw shadowy forms in the darkness of his room. He heard someone breathing, quiet shallow breaths. Suddenly, angry hands grabbed him, their fingers clutching his hair. A voice hissed, "I am sick to death of you, lazy dog! What have you done to deserve my house, my food, and my father's favor?"

Blood pounded in Brae's ears, like the feathery beat of a giant winged creature. He almost believed he could see the shadow of a monster whose beaked head and talons strained toward him, reaching, clutching, as though they would curl themselves around his body and crush him as a vulture crushes the bones of a rotting carcass.

Jiron motioned to someone standing outside. The door was thrown back against the wall, and four young men, all of them angry, all wielding wooden clubs, stormed into the room. Brae screamed and fell to the floor as the first blow struck. Blood stained the woven rug where he lay, his knees drawn up to his chest.

A dog barked, and someone shouted. The blows ceased. Quietly, the young men left the house without a backward glance, all but Jiron. "Get out," he commanded. "If you are here at daybreak, you will not live to see another day."

In the thick darkness, haunted by the deeper blackness of shadows that loomed against the night, Brae left the Port of Plenty. Too weak to stand, he crawled toward the bay, inching his way one painful stretch at a time, leaving bloody prints to mark the path of his retreat.

He found the rowboat that had brought him to these shores beached where he had left it, beneath the low branches of a cypress bush outlined faintly against the night.

The light of a lantern glowed from the deck of the *Seeking*. Brae kept his gaze on it as he pulled, slowly and painfully, at the oars.

Bitter tears burned his eyes as he thought of the warm blankets and baskets of food he had wasted in the Port of Plenty. Now he was returning to an empty ship. And he had no one to blame but himself. With little hope, he strained at the oars, but the outline of the ship was growing dimmer now, swimming in a misty haze. As Brae squinted into the distance, it slipped from his sight completely, and he lay motionless in the bottom of the boat, drifting, dreaming—vague, unconnected scenes that made no sense at all.

Thump. Thump. Brae became dimly aware of the sound. Reaching out, he found he was still slumped in the bottom of the rowboat. Blood soaked his torn clothing and matted his hair. His cheeks burned as salty water doused raw abrasions. Peering through painfully swollen eyes, he recognized the *Seeking*. He tried to stand, only to collapse against the bottom of the skiff. He tried again, reaching desperate hands toward the *Seeking*, but his knees buckled and he hit his head against the side of the boat as he sank back into it. The ship began to drift away. Brae's battered body shook with sobs.

As in a dream, he felt hands, small but strong, lift him. Though he saw no one, he became dimly aware that he stood—with a strength not his own. That was when he realized that the rowboat had moved forward once more to bump against the ship, where the Messenger stood at the rail, hands extended.

Brae tried to reach his arms up, as a child reaches for his father, but there was no strength left in them. He looked helplessly into the Messenger's kind face as the ship began to drift beyond his reach. Once again he felt the hands of one he could not see lift his arms and hold them fast, as the rowboat surged on the crest of a wave toward the *Seeking*. At last the Messenger's strong hands touched his, and Brae felt himself propelled from behind by an unseen presence and pulled gently aboard.

As Brae struggled to stand on the deck, he looked around in disbelief. There, before his eyes, was an abundant supply of food and water. A stack of warm blankets lay nearby.

"While you delayed your return," the Messenger said, "Grace came and supplied all that you need to continue your journey."

It was then that Brae noticed the woman who had followed him out of the rowboat onto the deck. She stood at the Messenger's side, her hand resting lightly on his arm. Her eyes were as blue as the waters of the deep, her fair skin flawless. Her hair, reaching past her shoulders, shone like spun gold. A blue sash reaching down to the hem of her long, flowing dress draped her small waist. Her eyes were warm with compassion as the wounded boy crumpled against the friend he had forgotten. The Messenger picked up a woolen blanket and wrapped it around Brae's shoulders.

The moon was high among the stars when Brae fell asleep that night. He dreamt that the Messenger visited a place that was far away and yet so near that he had merely to step into it, and that there he obtained a royal blue vase, trimmed with golden leaves and adorned on each side with slender curved handles. Lifting the vase high, he poured a drop of golden oil onto the tip of his finger. Gently, he touched the oil to the suffering boy.

"By the wounds of the Wounded One, you are healed," he whispered. The Messenger looked at Brae, sleeping the sleep of one whose strength has gone. Tenderly, he applied another drop of oil to the sleeping boy's wounds. "By his wounds…" he repeated. Brae's labored breathing grew quiet.

～

The Messenger climbed the stairs to the deck and stood at the railing, looking out into the darkness of the night, remembering the awful day.

The Wounded One was his friend. He walked and talked with him through the corridors of time. Always, he had known that he would slip out of the halls of the Other Kingdom and enter the Kingdom of Adawm. He had known that the Wounded One would suffer much, for the price of redemption would not be cheap.

Emperor Addar himself laid the plan before the dawn of time. He knew that he would suffer the agony of bereavement, as his own son, king of the Other Kingdom, exchanged his royal throne for the dusty paths in the Valley of E'ure—the place of sacrifice, the battlefield for the inhabitants of Adawm.

But to know and to experience are as different as the heat of the desert sun and the chill of the Arctic seas.

"I couldn't protect him," the Messenger lamented. "The Kingdom of Adawm was his treasure—and it was his choice to pay the price of its redemption. There was no other way."

CHAPTER 7

A Visit in the Night

The darkness of night yielded to a still greater darkness, an unnatural absence of light. The moon hid behind smoky clouds bunched together like chunks of charcoal in a cotton sack. Shadows, like beasts raised from the pit, known only from legend and the occasional sighting by those who have come under their power or fought against it, writhed and slithered across the sky.

Umbler spread his leathern wings, callused by the ravages of time. He delighted in the roar of thunder and the charge of electrical energy that illuminated his fierce countenance for a fraction of a second. The wolven, Lucacius, commander of Dagog's forces, loped along at Umbler's side, his fangs glistening wetly in the residual electricity from on high. His eyes were red as blood, his neck thick and shaggy. He threw back his enormous head and howled at the storm, exultant on this darkest of nights.

Whelters, snake-like creatures with the blood-sucking habits of the leech, attached themselves to the back of the wolven and the dragon and glowed like fireflies in the night. Some who watched the sky may have thought that they were aliens, and of course, they would have been right, for such creatures were not created for this world.

The Messenger watched them whirl away through the clouds. He knew where they were going. Whenever a traveler on the Sea of Life lost his way, Dagog often met with his followers at the Valley of E'ure, the place of death. He went there to gloat, to boast of his victory in the very spot where he had suffered his greatest defeat.

Suddenly, there was a flash of bright light, as white as the dress of a bride on her wedding day. Dazzling and pure, it shone through the night. It looked, at first, like the beam of a beacon such as one might see atop a lighthouse, a light to guide lost boats to safety on a troubled sea; then it began to condense, growing smaller but brighter. Finally, it took the shape of a dove, larger than most, but beautifully formed. The light dimmed as it entered the dove and was diffused, becoming a soft, warm glow shining from within the stately form.

The white dove lifted its wings and sailed into the smoky sky. As it flew, the storm clouds dissipated and the stars began to shine. The moon peeked out from behind the clouds and then rose above them to illuminate the sky and the sea. Still the dove ascended. Breaking through the ranks of stars, it entered the realm of the Other Kingdom. The Shining Warriors bowed before it, and a courier hastened to the throne room to announce its arrival. But the courier was too slow. Before he reached to steps of the royal palace, the dove had entered, made straight for the throne room, and alighted on the extended arm of Immon.

King Immon laughed at the courier whose astonished expression gave way to a delighted grin. "Everyone likes to be the bearer of good news," Immon said. "You have done well, my friend, but your general may have better use of your services than I at the moment."

As the courier hastened off, Immon turned to the dove resting lightly on his arm. He stroked the pure white feathers and looked into its golden-brown eyes. He did not address the bird directly, but those who stood by knew that he conversed with it—a long and intimate conversation—though no words were spoken. Between the dove and Immon words were unnecessary, for each knew the other's mind perfectly.

Emperor Addar, Ruler of Kingdoms, smiled. He too knew the language of the heart shared by Immon and the Dove. He laughed along with Immon when the dove commented on the journey of Dagog to the Valley of E'ure. His eyes twinkled and he reached an enormous hand to clap the knee of Immon. "Will the beast never learn that his victories are as empty as the grave?"

Immon lifted his arm and the dove took flight. It circled the thrones of Addar and Immon once, and again, and then was gone. Within moments it descended to the deck of the *Seeking*, where a former slave from the City of Bondage was just waking from a sound sleep.

CHAPTER 8

Umbler's Bright Idea

Umbler returned from the council in the Valley of E'ure with dragging wings. The meeting did not go well. Dagog was incensed at the failure of the trap in the Port of Plenty, and took his frustration out on his most convenient subject.

Umbler rubbed his aching head and tried to ignore the pain in his injured wing. He had known this assignment would not be easy, but he hadn't expected failure so soon.

Lucacius sat on his haunches across from the wounded dragon, grinning. He always enjoyed the failures of others. It was so inspiring, made him feel… superior. His smug expression irritated the dragon.

"Well, don't you have anything to say?" Umbler squirmed.

"You want me to say I told you so?" Lucacius raised one busy eyebrow and cocked his head to the side.

The dragon glared at his rival. "Dagog said you could give me some… pointers. This case is obviously not going according to our plan."

"Well…" Lucacius drawled, "perhaps you should ask for assistance from someone better… suited to the task."

Had the wolven been flesh and blood he would have been disintegrated by the glare of red-hot dragon eyes. But of course he was not, so he just grinned at the furious dragon that exhaled a ferocious black cloud in his direction. Lucacius sniffed the air. Sulfur. Delicious.

"I know just the right assistant for you," Lucacius suggested. "It takes a certain… skill… to succeed with the young ones. He will do the work and you will receive the credit. He will, after all, be your assistant."

The suggestion cheered the junior dragon. "Yes. You are exactly right, Commander." An ugly grin spread across Umbler's face, extending from the blue-green mole on the left side of his crooked mouth to the blood-red wart that dangled, like a worm on a hook, from his right cheek. His headache faded. Even his wounded wing felt a little better.

CHAPTER 9

A Perilous Companion

Young bones soon mend, and it was not long before Brae was up and about. Soon he was diving into the sea for a swim, climbing the rigging in search of land, and becoming quite bored. One day, he was in the crow's nest, telescope in hand, when he spotted a raft approaching. He laughed at the sight of it, for it was purple, like a big colored egg. The young man inside was having the time of his life, waving his hat and shouting each time the boat crested a wave, landing with a splash in the troughs between. He was headed straight for the *Seeking*. Brae did not notice that the shadow cast across the waves by the boy who stood whooping and waving did not fit his slender shape. Shadowed wings stretched wide across the foaming swells, cresting white—as if littered by downy feathers shed by some great bird.

"Hey!" Brae shouted, cupping his hands over his mouth. "You, over there. Come aboard."

A friendly grin spread across the tanned face of the youth in the boat. His long curly hair, black as soot, stirred in the morning breeze. Lifting his hand in a cocky salute, he squinted into the sun. "I'll be right there," he called.

In a few moments, the stranger had pulled alongside, lightly scrambled up a rope ladder, and vaulted over the rail. He winked at the Messenger, who stood, frowning, at the rail, and advanced toward Brae, a grin on his face and his hand outstretched.

"Hi," he bubbled. "I'm Damien."

"I'm Brae. Welcome aboard."

Looking around the ship and sniffing the aroma of soup cooking in the galley, Damien said, "Umm, something sure smells good."

Brae didn't wait for him to ask. "There's plenty," he said, looking at the Messenger for confirmation. The Messenger said nothing.

"Well, then." Brae ended the awkward silence. He clapped Damien on the shoulder. "Let's check the galley."

Damien bent over the soup that bubbled in the cast-iron pot, and then opened the oven door. "Cornbread!" He sounded as if he had just struck gold. "Let's eat."

Both boys grabbed bowls and filled them to the brim with soup. They scooped out chunks of red potato, squash, and tomato and heaped them onto plates.

"Hey," Brae grabbed Damien's hand, the first misgiving flitting like a startled bird across his thoughts. "Save some for the Messenger."

"Oh, I forgot about him," Damien said grimacing. He looked so comical, so chagrined, that Brae burst out laughing. Damien joined him.

The sun was sinking into the darkening sea when Brae realized that he and Damien had lingered at the table long past dinnertime and the Messenger must be starving. He kept looking for an opportunity to interrupt Damien without seeming rude. The soup had grown cold and the few pieces of cornbread left on the table seemed smaller than Brae had realized.

Finally, Brae jumped up and playfully punched Damien. "Hey, let's go on deck and you can take a turn at the wheel."

"Let's go!" Damien grinned.

When Brae went to bed that night, he neglected to say goodnight to the Messenger. In fact, he tiptoed past him, sneaking down the narrow stairs to his bunk. The Messenger, staring out to sea, appeared not to notice. Brae wondered what he was thinking.

Long after Brae fell asleep, the Messenger kept his vigil at the rail. Damien knew the reason for his diligent watch, even if Brae did not. The moon rose high in its arc to rest above the *Seeking*, casting its pale light on the water. Though aware of Damien's presence beside him before the deceiver had spoken a word, still the Messenger waited for him to speak.

"I will win, you know." Damien had discarded his boyish voice for this conversation. There was no need to pretend with the Messenger. His low growl would have made the hair stand up on Brae's neck if he could have heard it.

The Messenger did not bother to answer. Keeping his eyes fixed on the black water, he gripped the rail.

"He doubts you already," the hoarse whisper prodded. "He is mine...."

At the last word, the Messenger turned toward Damien. A light, brighter than the sun at high noon, shone from his eyes, burning into the black eyes of the deceiver. Damien threw his hands up to shield his face, and the flesh on the back of his hands began to shrivel. "No!" he begged as he fell to his knees. The Messenger turned away and resumed his watch.

Damien struggled to his feet and stumbled down the steps to his bed.

The following morning Damien rose and set out to find Brae. He laughed as the morning breeze ruffled his hair. Locating Brae on the bridge, taking a turn at the wheel, he called out, "Hey Brae! Let's grab some breakfast."

Brae grinned. Seeing Damien's bandaged hand, he asked, "Hey, what happened to you?"

Damien glanced at the Messenger moving closer to take the wheel. "I got hungry in the night. Tried to heat some soup but I guess I don't know how to work that old stove so well." He shrugged. "Don't worry, it's not as bad as it looks." Proud of his deception, he winked at the Messenger before taking off, with Brae right behind him, to scale the rigging.

Weeks passed with no sign of land. Brae thought they should at least have come in sight of an island by now. He wasn't very good at reading the maps just yet, but he was working on it.

One afternoon, Brae went to the rail to stand beside the Messenger. He missed talking with him. He seemed so distant, so aloof. *Maybe he's angry because I invited Damien aboard without asking him first.* Brae took a deep breath. He knew he should talk to his old friend, but he wasn't sure what to say.

"Is something wrong?" Brae asked.

"Yes," the Messenger answered quietly.

"Well?" Brae waited.

When the Messenger remained silent, Brae shrugged his shoulders and stomped away to find Damien. "What's the matter with him?" Brae glanced back at the Messenger, who stood with quiet dignity, like a soldier standing guard, and wondered again what the Messenger could see in the distance.

One day, Damien asked Brae, "Whom should we shoot at dinner tonight?"

Expecting one of Damien's crude jokes, Brae laughed. "I don't know."

"The Messenger," Damien replied, laughing at his own humor.

Brae wasn't laughing. "Why would you say that?"

"Hey, I was just joking," Damien answered. "You know, 'don't shoot the messenger….' "

But there was something in his eyes—something Brae had seen somewhere before. Somehow that *something* made being with Damien a lot less fun.

One day, the Messenger told Brae to stay off the rigging.

"Why?" he and Damien asked in unison.

"Because a southeast wind is coming up and the rigging is not safe in high winds."

The Messenger went below deck and sat in the galley, his eyes closed. He leaned on his elbows, hands folded in front of him. For a long time he sat in silence, head bowed. A narrow shaft of sunlight streamed through the porthole; it caressed his silver-gray hair, cascaded over his face, and set-tled on his hands. Strong hands, they were, and used to work. His hands had navigated the *Seeking* through countless storms that rose upon the Sea of Life, and had plucked many a sailor out of the debris of a ship wrecked upon submerged mountains.

"With these hands I can rescue the perishing and repair broken ships," he thought, "but never will I lift these hands to rescue or repair against the will of man."

A terrified scream above deck shattered the silence. The Messenger ran up the stairs just in time to catch Brae as he tumbled from the top of the rigging. The Messenger stumbled under the impact, still holding Brae in his arms.

"Are you all right?" he asked, concern darkening his eyes.

Struggling to recover his breath, Brae pushed himself away from the Messenger and stood up. "Yeah," he puffed and strode off.

The Messenger followed Brae to his bunk below deck. "What is the matter?" he asked.

"You jinxed that rigging, didn't you?" Brae accused. "Damien told me that you would put a curse on the rigging so that I would fall if I disobeyed you! That's what you did, isn't it? Well, isn't it?"

The Messenger stood up and left the room.

At dinner a couple of hours later, Damien did all the talking. Brae stared at his plate without eating. The Messenger ate his food in silence. Damien told one joke after another, never seeming to notice that he was the only one laughing. As he passed the Messenger going up the steps to the deck, he smirked at him behind Brae's back, a gesture the Messenger chose to ignore.

That night, Damien sat on Brae's bunk. "I still can't believe what the Messenger did to you." He bounced up and down on the bed, slapping his hands against the covers with a jerky rhythm as if playing a drum. "That he would almost kill you just to prove he was right! You know, I'm thinking about leaving this old hulk soon. Want to come with me in my raft? There's plenty of room for two."

Surprised, Brae looked at Damien. Leave the ship? He had never thought of abandoning the journey. He said nothing, but he felt as if there was a rock in the pit of his stomach. He turned on his side and snuffed out the candle. Maybe he would feel better in the morning.

Damien was up early the following day. "Hey, Brae!" He punched his arm. "Let's climb up into the crow's nest and see if we can spot some land."

The Messenger stood at the wheel, looking eastward. "No," he commanded. "You must not climb the rigging today."

When the Messenger went below deck, Damien made an obscene gesture at his back. Brae pretended not to notice, but it was getting harder to overlook Damien's disrespect. Brae started to climb. This time, even though Brae held his head as if he were looking up, he squinted down at Damien from the corner of his eye. He watched Damien go to the pole that held up the supporting beam beneath the crow's nest. He saw him slip out a bolt and then start on the next one. Damien was dismantling the beam so that the crow's nest would fall! By the time Brae knew for certain what Damien was doing, he was high in the air. Though he knew his words would be lost in the wind, he called out, "Help! Someone, help me!"

In a flash, the Messenger was above deck and had grabbed Damien. It appeared to Brae that a mighty rushing wind had wrapped itself around the startled youth, lifted him over the rail, and deposited him, shrieking and cowering, onto the floor of the purple raft.

Brae descended just in time to see Damien drift away. His hand was lifted—but Brae knew Damien well enough by now to know that he was not waving a fond farewell. Laughter, cruel and malevolent, emanated from the raft. Brae stared across the waves, terrified. The fiendish howls subsided as the craft drew near a huge dark shadow that rested upon the waves. The shadow lifted for a moment, and Brae realized that it hid a gigantic black ship.

Brae fell to his knees, bile rising in his throat. The huge ship seemed alive with thousands of eyes that glowered at him through the thickening mist. He caught his breath, feeling his stomach squeeze into a tight knot as his gaze traveled upward to spy the flagstaff high above the topmast. It bore the mark of the dragon and appeared drenched in blood, a crimson trail that seeped down the mast and stained both beam and sail.

The smell of sulfur and putrefying flesh gagged Brae. He leaned over the rail and lost his breakfast in the sea. At last, he grasped the rail with trembling hands and pulled himself to his feet.

The Messenger stood beside him. "The dragon ship *Avenger*," he said. "It is the flagship of Dagog's fleet. It has been following us for weeks."

"The *Seeking* is like a toy next to that… thing," Brae said, his voice trembling.

The Messenger's hand tightened on the rail. "Dagog will not be pleased when the purple raft returns without a captive."

"You knew who Damien was when he first came aboard?"

"I know him," The Messenger said. "He may appear young, but he has been in the service of Dagog for ages. He has deceived many people, luring them into his raft and then delivering them into the hands of his master."

Brae, for once, was silent. *I am so stupid*, he thought. He now hated Damien as much as he had liked him before.

The Messenger frowned. "I remember another young man. His name was Alex. He too welcomed Damien aboard his ship. Alex was eighteen and thought himself wise. After a few months of Damien's company, Alex jumped into the purple raft with him and turned his back on the Other Kingdom."

The Messenger strode to the wheel and altered course, taking the *Seeking* far away from the dragon ship.

CHAPTER 10

A Troubling Memory

The night breezes, cool and salty, swept through the rigging of the *Seeking*. Stars splayed across the heavenly canvas, illuminating the solitary ship sloshing through gentle seas. A perfect night for sleep and dreams.

But Brae did not sleep. He lay on his mattress, which he had taken to the observation deck, the floor above the cabin, where he hoped the breeze would lull him into slumber. Staring at the stars, he let himself return to the shadowy past, the earliest days of his captivity in the City of Bondage. Squeezing his eyes shut against the tears that slipped down his cheeks to soak the pillow beneath, he surrendered to memory and sank beneath it as one drowning, frightened and alone.

Darkness descended. Like a massive stone it pressed against Brae's chest. He drew quick shallow breaths. His stomach clenched and his hands curled into fists. A silvered screen unfolded and images began to play across it.

There was a man. He looked a lot like Brae, but older. Gray was beginning to show at his temples against his dark brown hair. His eyes were green as grass and his garments…

Brae realized with a start that the man was his father and he was not wearing slave apparel but the tunic worn by nobility. The man turned to look at the woman beside him and his face was transformed by tenderness. He took her arm as one might hold a priceless treasure. And then he looked at the child.

Brae knew, somehow, that the child, an infant snuggled in the woman's arms, was himself. The child fisted its tiny hands and cried as the mother yielded it to another who stood by, a young girl in the garb of a slave. The mother's hands lingered on the child, stroking his face, touching his hands. Someone shoved her, ordering her to move along. She stumbled forward, supported by the man at her side, who wept openly as the mother fainted in his arms.

The slave girl turned away from the couple, her face hard as stone. Brae drew a quick breath as he recognized the matron, the slave who bore responsibility for the welfare of children born and raised in the house of Meriquoi.

Then Brae noticed the chains that bound his parents to each other and to those who stood in line behind them, waiting to board a ship. Brae wrenched his gaze from his father's face and studied the ship, which bore a remarkable resemblance to the *Seeking*.

But how can this be? The Messenger is in charge of the emperor's ships, and he would force no one to sail with him. And to bind them with chains—this is not the Messenger's work.

How do you know? The familiar voice of Doubt nagged at Brae. *He sent you ashore at the Port of Plenty and look what happened to you there. Perhaps the Messenger is crafty. Nothing is as it seems.*

The silver screen vanished and Brae opened his eyes. Soot-gray clouds had rolled in from the east and the air had chilled. A tinge of crimson streaked the sky. Brae thought of the bloody flag atop the *Avenger* and shuddered.

CHAPTER 11
Umbler Rebuked

"That was not good." Lucacius wagged his shaggy head from side to side. "We give you a simple assignment and you fail, outsmarted by a *slave boy*!" Lucacius spat the last word out of his mouth with distaste.

Umbler cringed, the dingy white feathers at the crown of his neck drooping. He sat, shoulders hunched, facing the wolven. A mist rose from his sweaty wings.

Lucacius sniffed. The fragrance of fear always excited the wolven. He licked his paw, allowing a bit of drool to trickle down his chin. "Do you wish to abdicate?"

"No!" Umbler was not ready to plead. "I have… an idea."

"Yes?" Lucacius waited.

"Yes," Umbler said, thinking fast. "A storm. We could stir up a storm."

The sound of Lucacius' laugh was not pleasant. "Do you really think you can do that?" he asked.

"Dagog—"

"Don't even think about it." Lucacius lay on the ground, his massive head resting on his paws, eyebrows tilted in disdain. "What do they teach these beasts in school these days?" he muttered half under his breath.

"What—?"

"Dagog cannot just whip up a storm like a child making bubbles in a bathtub." Lucacius' lips curled in disgust.

"Then how—?" Umbler wished Lucacius would let him finish just one sentence.

"Dagog storms through the heavens, leaving a wake of wounded clouds behind. The warriors of the sky see the disturbance and war against our master. Sometimes the emperor Himself comes down. He rides on the wings of the wind." Lucacius' eyes glowed red. "Dagog has fallen from heaven more than once in the tempest of the Emperor's wrath. But if you ever speak of it…"

"What do you suggest, most favored General?" Umbler mumbled. Now he was ready to plead.

"You must not—I repeat, must not—under any circumstances allow the subject to accept the Certificate of Redemption provided by Immon to those recruited by Mercy at the Cape of Conviction." Lucacius pointed toward a sandy shore rising out of the sea mists. "Do you see it yonder?"

Umbler nodded, unable to squeeze even the smallest sound through his constricted throat.

"You'd better think of something!" Lucacius tossed over his shoulder as he turned away from the junior dragon and sprinted off to find his master.

Umbler sat back on his tail, eyes closed, thinking with all his might.

CHAPTER 12

The Trial

At midmorning several weeks later, Brae began to feel a strange foreboding. The sun grew dark and a dreary rain began to fall. He saw a murky shoreline through the mist that swirled across the restless waves.

"That," the Messenger said quietly, "is the Cape of Conviction."

As they drew closer, Brae could see the dingy buildings of a small town with an enormous masonry structure in the center of it. Squinting through the billowing mists, he saw that it had once been a prison; but was vacant now, its buttresses crumbling. The iron bars on the windows bled rusty stains down the sides of the formidable edifice. Huge iron balls attached to thick chains lay strewn around a courtyard behind tall wrought-iron gates. In the entryway a number of machines clearly designed for torture stood deteriorating, worn with age and much use.

The sign above the portico had come loose on one side and now reclined at an angle against a ragged awning over the doorway. "Condemned" was emblazoned in faded lettering against a once-white background.

Brae wondered why the prison was abandoned. Had there been a rebellion that had overcome the prison guards and freed the prisoners?

He preferred to go around this strange place, but something compelled him to anchor his ship and go ashore.

As soon as he set foot on land, Brae was surrounded by an angry mob. They swarmed from the ancient courthouse that rested on a solid rock beside the crumbling prison. The weathered stone building appeared strong, supported by the enormous rock on which it was built. The statue of a woman, crafted in bronze, graced the entrance to the massive building, which bore the inscription Department of Justice. With a somber frown, she scrutinized those who passed by, watching in silence as the execution of justice was carried out.

Someone grabbed Brae's shirt and ripped it from his back. Another reached out a strong hand and locked iron shackles around his wrists. A stooped old man took a rope from a bag that hung at his side and wrapped it around Brae's ankles. He was then dragged before a tall, severely thin man dressed in black judicial robes. A wooden gavel rested on the bench before him.

"Fall to your knees in the presence of Justice!" a loud voice commanded.

Brae did so.

"Read the charges against this man," the voice said.

The judge picked up a thick scroll. As he unrolled it, Brae could see that it was very long and many things had been written on it. Brae was aghast. He had been a good man. How could he have broken the law? He trembled as he heard his crimes read aloud.

The judge began: "You, Brae—of the City of Bondage—are accused of living entirely for yourself without any regard to the harm you may have caused others. You are accused of omitting to do that which was good, because you were unconcerned for the welfare of other people. In particular, you are accused..."

The list went on interminably. It included every unkind word Brae had ever spoken, every lie he had told, every cruel deed that had hurt someone else, and every act of selfishness. Brae closed his eyes. *There is no hope for me*, he thought. *I am guilty!*

"Finally," the judge said, "you are accused of contributing to the death of the only blameless person to ever trod the soil in the Kingdom of Adawm. Your crime is punishable by death."

Falling on his face, Brae cried out for mercy!

The crowd was silent as a man with a deeply lined face and snow-white hair approached the bench. He was a good twelve inches shorter than Brae but seemed much taller. His shoulders were straight, his eyes kind.

"I am Mercy," he said.

Brae's accusers bowed their heads. Without a word, Mercy took Brae by the hand and led him out of the building and along the streets to a place just outside the town.

Brae followed Mercy without protest, hesitating only when they reached the end of the path and stopped before a vast, low-lying hill.

"This is the Hill of Death," Mercy said.

Rows and rows of white tombstones stood in solemn dignity against the gray clouds, monuments to those whose lives had passed. On the rounded peak of the Hill of Death, a mammoth silver birch tree raised its limbs to embrace the sky.

Mercy waved his hand toward the living monument. "This tree," he said, "is the place of execution and a monument to the one who died in your place."

"Why would anyone do that?" Brae was incredulous.

"The story is told in the *Ancient Book of Mysteries*," Mercy answered. "Have you not read it?"

Brae looked down. How could he tell Mercy that he had disdained the book, had tried to ignore it though he knew that it was intended to guide him on his way to the Other Kingdom.

"Let us say—" Mercy looked into Brae's eyes with an intensity that frightened him "—that One who did no wrong had such a great and enormous heart that he could not enjoy the benefits of the Other Kingdom without giving everything that he had to provide a second chance to those condemned to die. Does this interest you?"

"I don't understand it," Brae answered honestly.

"Well said." Mercy nodded his head with a vigor that startled Brae. "You will not understand until you accept the gift. You are still in Dagog's service."

"Not Dagog. I will not serve him."

"You believe that you have a choice?" Mercy thundered. His hair, electrified by his passion, stuck out in all directions. His eyes, so kind just moments before, burned with the fire of his conviction. "You can serve the great King Immon or you can serve Dagog, but you must serve one or the other—because to fail to serve the one is to choose the other."

"I cannot choose." Brae's tortured voice betrayed the turmoil he experienced. He stood at the parting of two ways and had no way of knowing the cost of choosing one over the other.

"The Wounded One offers you his life," Mercy said. "It is a free gift."

"How can this be?" Brae asked. "Where I come from, nothing is free."

"The gift is free, but it has been purchased for you at great cost," Mercy said.

"So it will cost me nothing?" Brae asked.

Mercy shook his head. "How can you not understand?" Then he answered his own question. "Your eyes are blinded to the Truth, young Brae. Close your eyes."

Brae did so.

"What do you see?"

"I see a garden. It is as large as a city. It must be nearing harvest, for the produce is ripe."

"If I give you this field without exacting payment, is the field a free gift?"

"Yes!" Brae answered.

"Will it cost you anything?"

"No," Brae replied. "It is a gift."

"But if you accept this gift—then you must cultivate the soil in the spring and then plant the seeds. You must weed the fields throughout the summer and stand guard over the tender fruit. It will be your responsibility to reap the harvest. And then you can enjoy the fruit of your labor. Does this cost you anything?"

"It costs me everything," Brae answered.

Mercy nodded.

CHAPTER 13

Umbler Scores a Victory

"D o something!" Umbler squealed, wishing he had the courage to strike the grin from the face of his commander. "You're supposed to help me!"

His fists were clenched at his side, his wings folded beneath his feathered cloak. Rising up from the ashes of his defeat, he took a step toward the wolven and tripped over a rotten log. His legs flew upward, talons clutching at the wind, and he landed on his face in the muck. Squinting through the sticky ooze, nostrils flared, he blew his breath out in heaving gasps. "Dagog ordered you to instruct me," he seethed, embarrassment clouding his judgment.

A snarl instantly replaced the grin on the wolven's face, and he whirled away from Umbler. "You'd better watch yourself," he growled.

Umbler stood his ground. "Well... ?"

"All right, this is how it will be." Lucacius forgot his disdain for Umbler as he began to plot the demise of the subject. Coconspirators once again, the dragon and the wolven schemed the night away. For it was night in the domain of the Prince of the Darkness, though in the Kingdom of Adawm the sun peeked through the mist and the clouds; and time, it seemed, stood still.

CHAPTER 14

Beneath the Silver Birch Tree

B rae stared at the ancient silver birch tree that towered high above the Hill of Death. It cast its shade over all that lay beneath. Birds, thousands of them, rested in its branches, their voices raised in harmonious song. Silver-green heart-shaped leaves, the size of a man's hand, fluttered in the breeze, emitting a fragrance that was at once exciting and soothing.

Brae wanted to embrace the tree, to throw his arms around its massive trunk and breathe deeply of its aroma. Somehow, he expected to find its trunk warm, responsive to his embrace. But something deterred him— a premonition that if he did so, he would be forever changed, that the tree would become a part of himself, or he a part of the tree.

"Stop!"

Brae looked around, hearing the command, but saw no one.

The speaker once again intruded, as if from within his head. "This is crazy! You have been brought here to die! Run! Get away from this place as fast as you can!"

Fear overwhelmed Brae, flooding him with doubt. Distrust, his old familiar companion, swept away the fragile longing that drew him to the tree. He took a step backward.

"You are not ready to die." The voice was louder now, more confident. "You were a slave but now you are free."

Determination seized Brae. "I will not give up my freedom." Suddenly, he hated this place! He jerked away from Mercy and began to run. He zigzagged between the tombstones and plunged into the surrounding forest, then circled around, heading for the beach.

The sun was low over the emerald waters of the Sea of Life when Brae climbed into his rowboat and returned to the *Seeking*. He glanced back toward the land, amazed that he could still see the silver birch that stood upon the hill, enveloped in the crimson light of the setting sun.

Far away in the Other Kingdom, Emperor Addar and his son, King Immon, known to many as the Wounded One, sat upon their thrones, watching through a curtain of cloud as Brae fled the Cape of Conviction. In his hand, Immon held a parchment that bore the name "Brae, former slave of Meriquoi." At the top was the heading "Certificate of Redemption."

Addar patted his son's hand. "You are disappointed."

"The young believe time belongs to them." Immon shook his head. "Dagog knows better. The trap has been set."

~

Umbler danced upon the clouds, "Yes, yes, yes…" he exulted. "I did it. I'm the best." Fantasies of reveling in his master's pleasure had his head spinning until he bumped into Lucacius just as the wolven was coming out of a billowing thunderhead. Umbler blinked, unprepared for the hard smack the irritated wolven delivered to his grinning face.

"What did you do that for?" he asked, rubbing his chin, careful not to disturb the wart that dangled from his cheek. Every time it wiggled Lucacius mocked him, and Umbler had experienced enough ridicule from his commander. He would not allow Lucacius to steal his thunder—not this time.

"You fool," Lucacius growled, and Umbler began to suspect that the wolven's anger had nothing to do with getting bumped. His glee melted.

"What?" Umbler tried unsuccessfully to keep the tremor from his voice.

"Dagog is about to… relieve you of your responsibilities." Lucacius seemed pleased to deliver the news.

"Why? I don't—"

"Shut up, you fool!"

Umbler shut his mouth so quickly that he severed the tip of his tongue. He didn't dare open his mouth to spit. Lucacius looked ready to explode, his eyes wild, his hackles raised. Umbler tasted blood. He swallowed hard, gagging on the bitterness of his disappointment.

Head sagging, Umbler waited. Lucacius seemed in no hurry to speak.

"You let him see the tree." The wolven advanced, slowly, deliberately, toward the cowering dragon. "You let him hear the Truth. Do you think this is a victory?"

"He listened to me," Umbler said. "Why do you think—"

"That he didn't bend the knee?" Lucacius finished, his hot breath foul in the dragon's face. "Because he still thinks as a slave. Because the City of Bondage still resides within him. And possibly, because of your words in his head. But your words were entirely inadequate. He has seen the tree, felt its power. Do you think he will forget? You are a fool."

Umbler's head sank lower into his hunched shoulders, and blood drizzled from the corners of his mouth. He raked a hand across his face, accidentally setting off the inflamed wart. Like the silent tolling of a bell, it swung first to the left and then to the right.

Lucacius fixed his eyes upon the wart, distracted, irritated by the movement. A movement he could not control... unless...

In one swift move, he leapt at the face of the despairing dragon, clamped his teeth upon the offending wart, and bit down—hard.

"Eeeeeeeeee," Umbler's agonized squeal echoed through the corridors of Darkness. The wart may have been ugly, and a nuisance at times, but it in the world of Darkness it was sign of his stature. He had been robbed. Howling, the dragon fell on his face.

After a time he sat up, swiped the blood from his cheek, and resolved that Brae, former slave of Meriquoi, his first *subject* in the Kingdom of Adawm, would pay for this. Suddenly, his suffering had purpose. Umbler, junior dragon in the service of Dagog, felt his wings stiffen. He raised them high, catching a swift current as it swept past. He had work to do.

Bill of Rights and Ancient Creed
of the Land of Lasciviousness

In this Land,
Lasciviousness
Is the Order of the Day.
No one forces others
To do as one may say.
But all are free to dress, or not,
To come and go at will,
To be the person that will please
Himself and no one else.
Lasciviousness, you may have heard
Is evil. Poppycock!
Superstitions such as this
Are not for the evolved.

By our Law:

All should live uncensored
By a public-minded view
Whatever is right in your own eyes
Is the righteous thing to do.

CHAPTER 15

Land of Lasciviousness

The Messenger was quiet when Brae returned from the Cape of Conviction. He seemed disappointed. *What did he expect me to do?* Brae fumed. He felt irritable and avoided the Messenger whenever he could do so.

Late one evening, Brae sighted land. He was so tired of sailing; he couldn't wait to get his feet on the ground. He tugged at the ropes securing the rowboat. *Why can't I get it loose?* he thought, frowning in irritation.

The Messenger came to stand beside him. "Where are you going?"

"Obviously, I'm going ashore," Brae muttered.

"There is danger on this island," the Messenger warned. "It is called the Land of Lasciviousness—"

"I don't see anything wrong with it," Brae interrupted, refusing to look toward the shoreline, vaguely visible through the thick mist. Shrill laughter, the artificial kind that one hears often in rowdy clubs, pierced the haze, and music—loud and chaotic—boomed across the water, echoing against the sides of the *Seeking*.

Ignoring the Messenger's concerned gaze, Brae turned abruptly and launched the boat, rowing hard toward the island. Invisible fingers covered his ears so that he could not hear the mocking laughter that cackled through the sky as the monster lifted its wings to glide behind the clouds. Umbler roared his pleasure.

Pulling ashore, Brae watched a group of people dancing around a fire that flamed high against the sky, their naked bodies glistening with perspiration and strangely perfumed oil, strong and sweet.

By the time he approached the fire, Brae's feet were moving with the music. Soon he was leaping and shouting along with the natives as they worshipped the fire and paid homage to the god of the night.

Intent upon the dance and the dancers around him, Brae did not see that the Messenger had followed him ashore and now watched him from the shadows. The Messenger's wise eyes looked beyond the flailing arms and legs of the dancers and the leering faces of the men who sat cross-legged at the fire. Looking deeper, he could see the disease rotting a young man's heart as he laughed and lusted after forbidden fare.

Unheeded, the Messenger turned away to walk among the inhabitants of the Land of Lasciviousness. Even here, in this wicked realm, the light would shine in the morning.

CHAPTER 16

A Gift Bestowed

The Messenger stood before Emperor Addar.

"You have come from the Land of Lasciviousness," the emperor said.

The Messenger nodded.

Addar stood before his throne. "Immon has spoken for our child who stumbles in the darkness."

"Brae has been deceived by Umbler, servant of Dagog. He stumbles in the Darkness but he will soon recover," the Messenger predicted. "I have sent Suffering to visit him. Suffering is the greatest of our teachers."

"And what of the Land of Lasciviousness? What have you seen there?"

"Everywhere I went throughout that land, I saw enslaved people, bound with great chains to Dagog. Everywhere they go they drag their chains with them. They grow incredibly weary, but they do not understand why. They do not even seem to be aware that they are in chains.

"This seemed strange to me. Why could they not feel the weight of the iron, the chafing of their flesh? How could they ignore the bruising tugs against their limbs by the monster that enslaves them? And then I realized that they all draw their water from a stagnant pool in the center of the land, a foul-smelling swamp the inhabitants of the land call 'Dagog's well.' I discerned that this numbs and seduces them so that they cannot see what is in plain sight right before them."

"They are intoxicated by pleasure, terrified by the truth," said the emperor.

"It is time." Immon rose from his throne and crossed the room. He opened the door to an adjoining room, allowing a stream of amber light to flood the throne room. He stepped inside. Around the walls were shelves of mother of pearl attached to the wall by golden brackets. The shelves held vases of exquisite pottery and crystal vials, some overlaid with precious metals, and others adorned with rubies, sapphires, and diamonds. But the outward beauty of the vessels was meager compared to the value of their contents.

Immon selected a small vial and returned to his throne. The Messenger stood, waiting.

Will I never cease to tremble when Immon places the vial in my hand? he thought, staring at the object that lay in the center of his palm. The vial felt warm in his hand and radiated a soft golden light, like the light that shone from the silver birch tree embossed on the cover of the *Ancient Book of Mysteries*.

"Go now!" Immon resumed his throne. "The time is short."

Holding the vial firmly, the Messenger nodded and stepped backward.

In the days that followed, the Messenger visited every dwelling in the Land of Lasciviousness, even those hidden deep in the forest. Those who welcomed him would never be the same, for the Messenger spoke to them the words of the *Ancient Book of Mysteries*, and the life that flowed through the words like a living light warmed their hearts. He reached out his hand to touch their eyes and the blinders fell from them. They now saw the monster that they had been chained to for so many years, and wondered that they were alive. The wild eyes and frenzied fury of the beast sent spasms of terror through their hearts. They gagged at the white flecks of foam that clung to his sooty cheeks, choked on the stench of his breath. They struggled with all their might to free themselves from the chains that bound them to the monster, but found the effort futile. When their arms failed them and their strength was spent, then they were ready.

They came to the Messenger as a moth flutters to the light. Fragile, helpless, and afraid, they came, no longer frightened by death but terrified by the beast that consumed them. They trembled as the Messenger said, "This is the oil of the silver birch tree that stands on a hill in the Cape of Conviction. The tree is a monument to the One who died there with great and terrible suffering. By his blood he paid the price, and by his life he offers pardon to all those who acknowledge their need of it. It is reserved for those who have been tried and found guilty of treason, as you have, one and all. By the touch of this oil, you will enter into his suffering, and through the passage of his suffering you will be pardoned. If this is your desire, then bend your knees and receive the free gift that was provided for you at unspeakable cost to Immon, your king and rightful ruler over this land.

As they did so, their heavy chains fell away, like dried leaves disintegrating into powder before a great wind. Like children born anew from the womb of death, they laughed and danced, hugged each other and cried.

There was one among them who felt their joy and rejoiced with them, but his joy was tempered by knowledge of the suffering that awaited the servants of Immon in the Land of Lasciviousness. He would be there in the midst of it, would feel their pain, experience their sorrow. But intervene he would not, for that is the way of the Kingdom. The fellowship of suffering, while excruciating to those who enter into it, is the pathway to intimacy with the Wounded One, who suffered more than any who came before or who will come after him in the Kingdom of Adawm. And those who enter the fellowship of His suffering will find that for each cup of pain endured in his service there is an ocean of joy stored up for the sufferer in the Other Kingdom.

CHAPTER 17
Sadie

S he was bent and wrinkled. Even in her youth she had attracted few admirers and had long ago resigned herself to a solitary life, alone in a miserable hovel at the edge of the land. Sadie had no stomach for the rituals of fire or the feasts of pleasure. She had won her small self-respect in the only way she could—by becoming a seer. And for this she was well known and sometimes feared.

She had watched the young man, Brae, from the shadows since the day he stepped ashore. She despised his deceptive charm, which soon dissipated among the inhabitants of the land as she had known it would, but there was still something about him... some seeking, some vulnerability... that touched a tender spot in her otherwise hardened heart.

I cannot learn his secret by listening to the boy, she thought. *For he is consumed already by this land and is not himself. I will follow the one who came in his shadow.* She had noticed that the Messenger appeared immediately after Brae, and she alone had noted that no boat had borne him to shore. Sadie had seen a white dove, as large almost as an eagle, alight—not in the trees but in the shadow of the trees—and she believed, though she would dare to tell no one, that the Messenger had come to the land in the form of a beautiful white dove.

Once, he caught her staring at him. She looked away, expecting rejection or ridicule. In that brief glance she knew that this Messenger was no ordinary man. For the first time in her seventy-eight years Sadie experienced love. The eyes that met hers for a fraction of a second were like no other. Something long frozen in Sadie's heart began to thaw, just around the edges. Emotions that had been denied flooded over her, and she turned away and shuffled back to her hovel as fast as her arthritic feet could carry her. Sitting before her fire, she took out a long wooden pipe, filled it with the dried cikato grass, and puffed away until long after the stars and the moon had circuited the sky. And then she had gone in search of the Messenger.

And now, here she was, rising from bended knee to stand before him. The old seer stood silently. Words, her only trade, forsook her. He reached out and wrapped an arm around Sadie. "My daughter," he said, "do you understand what has happened to you today?"

Sadie nodded. Then, as if a well of living water gushed from the depths of her being, bringing life to the dormant seeds of hope and unexpected joy, Sadie burst into song:

> She who had no purpose
> Who wandered all alone
> Has been found of the King
> Who sits on His throne.
> For seventy-eight years
> I have wandered in fear
> In darkness and hatred
> And never a tear.
> The life I have wasted
> Is given anew
> Immon, my great King
> I give my life to You.

A little girl began to clap her hands. She stood beside her parents, who also began to clap. Then others joined in. Shouts of "Yay!" and "Hurrah!" rose from the lips of all. Men, women, and children encircled the old woman; some touched her shoulder, her arm, while others hugged her, their tears mingling with hers.

When they all stepped back, Sadie stood in the center of a circle of friends. "Oh, Sadie," the little girl said, "you are so beautiful!"

And indeed Sadie was. Her skin, though wrinkled, glowed softly as if touched by the sun. Her eyes sparkled, and the color, blue as the waters of the deep, was so intense that one could almost fall into it. And Sadie's smile transformed her plain face into a cameo of goodness.

The following day, the little girl, whose name was Salina, came to visit Sadie, and was once again amazed. For the miserable hovel where the old woman had lived for so long had been transformed. The floors were swept clean and the dishes were washed and put away. A sweet fragrance, like the oil of the silver birch tree, permeated the house. Sadie welcomed the girl, who returned often to sit at her feet and learn her trade, the skillful use of words that would benefit her greatly in the trials to come.

CHAPTER 18

Chief Sodomon

T hose who had been freed from their chains met each night in a clearing deep in the forest. Others who knew of their clandestine meetings were both envious and angry. They sensed their freedom and wanted to have it, but did not want to give up their pleasures. They called those who followed the Messenger "Resisters." The name seemed to fit.

Their leader, Surice, was an old man who had suffered long in the Land of Lasciviousness. He had been a rebel from the start. At the age of six he was punished for refusing to dance to the fire god. At twelve he was beaten for refusing to follow the rites of manhood, which demanded that he join his fellows in a ritual so lewd that to describe it would be improper.

Surice was happier than most citizens in the Land of Lasciviousness, for he made his home in the forest and rarely entered the city. A crystal stream that flowed past his humble hut offered pure, sweet water, and he married and raised his family in the relative peace of the deep woods.

When the Messenger arrived, Surice was the first to respond to his invitation. A Resister already, he welcomed both the Messenger and his message.

Late at night, while the forest lay draped in darkness, over a hundred Resisters huddled close around a forbidden fire, seeking warmth and comfort—warmth because the night was chilly; comfort, because death, like the shadow of a great bird of prey, hovered over them. "One day," Surice said, "death will swoop down upon us, and we will be transported to live forever in the Other Kingdom."

The Resisters were lawbreakers, every one. It had been decreed in ages past that all citizens in the Land of Lasciviousness must prove their allegiance to the Prince of the Darkness by the ritual dance. It was required that they shed their clothes and dance before the fire to the god of the night.

The Resisters, who pledged their allegiance to Immon, refused to dance—refused to pay homage to the Prince of the Darkness.

Chief Sodomon, ruler of the Land of Lasciviousness, sat inside his tent deep in conversation with one who visited often at the fire of the Resisters.

"They believe," the spy reported, "that a great King, Immon, is at war with one called Dagog, who rules over the Kingdom of Adawm, including the Land of Lasciviousness. They say this ruler is evil, and they oppose him. They believe that you are under the rule of Dagog."

"Therefore, they oppose me!" Furious, Sodomon turned pale. Few had dared challenge his authority. Wrapping his robe closer to his body, he stood, pacing before the fire that burned in the center of his dwelling, casting strange shadows. The forms of wolvens, whelters, and other ancient Mystics crept, slithered, and floated along the stained leather walls as the flames flickered.

"Evil!" Sodomon spat the word from his mouth. "A superstition. Those who speak of evil speak only to condemn others." After a brief silence, Sodomon continued. "By refusing to dance before the fire, these Resisters condemn those who do."

"Onidah!" the spy hissed through a toothless smirk. "They commit onidah." Already he could taste blood. He began to quote the ancient creed.

> "All should live uncensored
> By a public-minded view
> Whatever is right in your own eyes
> Is the righteous thing to do."

"Harmony in the Land of Lasciviousness depends upon the inherent right of every person to do what is right in his own sight without censure or condemnation," the spy whined.

His contorted face appeared hideous to Sodomon as the spy quoted the remedy of law. "He who censures the actions of another is guilty of onidah and shall be put to death." His thick lips twisted, and he licked them repeatedly, like a lizard about to feast.

"And death it shall be." Sodomon stopped his pacing and turned toward the shadowy forms that lined the wall like ethereal witnesses. "I will strip them of their clothes and force them to dance. And if they refuse, they will die."

Sodomon's face felt hot, and the heat in his hut seemed oppressive.

He stepped outside and relished the cool breeze sweeping through the fruited palms. He plopped down in the lush grass in front of his shelter, feeling quite pleased with himself. He looked up—into the face of the Messenger. Fear gripped his heart. Those eyes! They seemed to penetrate the flesh and see into his soul. As if looking into a mirror, Chief Sodomon trembled as he stared into the diseased cauldron of lust, hatred, and filth that consumed him. Then, like a mirror breaking, the image shattered. Chief Sodomon stood up and spat on the ground at the Messenger's feet. He turned away and promptly forgot what manner of man he was.

The Messenger resumed walking and was soon obscured by the foliage at the edge of the forest.

"I know where you are going," Sodomon fumed, "you and your... Resisters, hiding like vermin in the night!"

Watching the bushes close behind the Messenger, Sodomon realized that he hated him—more than he hated the rival chief who had killed his brother, more than the woman who had deserted him after two years of marriage. All of his hatred suddenly had focus. This man was an enemy above all others. Sodomon wanted to flay him alive before the entire village, to make his death an example.

But he knew that he wouldn't. He feared the Messenger too much.

CHAPTER 19

A Conference in the Other Kingdom

Addar was seated on his throne; Immon sat beside him, gazing into the distance. His jaw tightened. The old scars on his back tingled, reminding him of his suffering in the Kingdom of Adawm.

Addar looked into the Land of Lasciviousness. His eyes blazed with anger. Standing, he raised his hand against the land. Chief Sodomon, pacing before his fire as he plotted the death of innocent men, women, and children, stood on the brink of destruction. Molten fire, like lava, began bubbling up from the depths of the earth. The land trembled. The ground beneath Chief Sodomon's feet grew warm, then hot. A crevice began to open.

"No!" Immon stood to face his Father, his hand on Addar's shoulder. Indicating the Certificate of Redemption he held in his hand, he insisted, "He is mine, Father. Look." He motioned to a translucent being standing like a soldier at attention, his golden hair brushing his broad shoulders. "Andrae, start the scene."

Addar watched the replay of Chief Sodomon's life. There he was, a little boy, maybe five years old. He was crying, running the gauntlet. Older warriors with ugly symbols drawn on their faces mocked the child. "Cry, little baby girl!" they shouted. Stones were hurled, bruising the youngster. His tears turned to anger, and when he reached the end of the gauntlet, he seized an old woman by the hair and threw her to the ground.

"Mother," he hissed. "You should not have taught me to be weak. You should have taught me not to cry."

"A little more time," Addar agreed.

Addar sat down. Immon took his place beside him.

"Tomorrow," Addar said, "the Messenger sails for other lands."

"He has won many followers in the Land of Lasciviousness." Immon counted those huddled around the fire.

"They will not be discouraged," Addar predicted. "The Messenger has touched their eyes."

"So they see beyond the veil." Immon completed Addar's thought, as he often did. "Just like our followers in ancient times who were thrown to the lions, torched, and mutilated—but whose spirits escaped the edge of the sword, escaped unscathed into the Other Kingdom."

Addar settled back on his throne. Immon closed his eyes, imparting strength to those who lived under threat of death in the Land of Lasciviousness.

CHAPTER 20
A Sad Farewell

T he Messenger stood with his back to the fire, his head bowed. His followers rose and ran to him, embracing him. A little girl with black braids that hung to her waist clung to him, sobbing.

The Messenger lifted her in his arms. "Salina," he whispered "do not fear. I will never forsake you."

Salina cried, "But you said we won't see you at our fires. You are going away!"

"Salina," the Messenger said, "do you see the wind?"

The child shook her head. Her enormous eyes were fixed on his with the kind of intensity that is uncomfortable to all except small children.

"Do you see the love that fills your heart?"

Again, the child shook her head. "No."

"But you know that it is there. Even so, know that I am with you always."

Handing the child to her father, the Messenger turned from them and disappeared into the forest. There he knelt beside a mossy stone and sobbed, his shoulders heaving, tears falling like great drops of rain. He agonized over the suffering that the Resisters would soon endure. He willed them to be strong.

He stood up and turned toward the village. Dry leaves crumbled beneath his feet, and twigs snapped from the trees as he pushed his way through the woods. Things had changed in the Land of Lasciviousness. A drought had settled in, turning the forests brown and the crops to dust. The once prosperous land had become gaunt, cadaverous.

Standing in the shadows, the Messenger could see the great fire in the heart of the village and the figures dancing round it. There among them was the one who had forsaken his journey. "Why would this young man, once freed from the tyranny of Meriquoi, choose to live like this?" The Messenger grieved. "The classic case of a dog returning to his vomit."

The Messenger watched as a figure in a gray robe emerged from the darkness. He stood over seven feet tall. A pointed hood covered his head and most of his face. The Messenger looked grim. He knew this stranger's name—it was Suffering. Even in a crowd, he was hard to miss, yet Suffering sought no recognition. Only those who have been introduced know him. And those who have never forget.

Brae danced beside the fire with his usual companions. His sightless eyes did not see the hooded figure approach him. Like a supple willow branch, Suffering bent from the waist and whispered something in the boy's ear. Brae continued to dance as if he hadn't heard, so Suffering tapped him on the shoulder. Startled, Brae jumped to the right, knocking Surgie, nephew of Sodomon, to the ground. Surgie grabbed a handful of small stones and hurled them in Brae's direction. Someone else grabbed a club and took a swing at Surgie. He missed, and the club hit the person standing next to Surgie. A look of amazement spread over the poor man's face just before he went down, blood spurting from a gash on his forehead.

Brae moved away from the fire, melting into the shadows. Too late. An enraged man wielding a wooden club turned on him. "You are the cause of all this trouble," he said. "You bring bad luck. We should never have let you dance at our fire."

"Yes!" others agreed.

Chief Sodomon appeared, his wrath fueled by the wilted crops in the fields and the assault on his nephew. "Bind him!" he ordered. "Throw him into the stone house. We will burn him in the fire at sunrise. Perhaps when his body lies in ashes the rains will come…"

CHAPTER 21

A Second Chance for Umbler

T here was revelry in the middle clouds. The master himself, having returned from one of his many journeys, occupied a towering column of sodden clouds. His subjects gathered round him like a flock of vultures hungry for plunder.

Stretching out his arm, Dagog extended a soot-blackened hand toward his minions. All fell down before him.

"Arise, my servants," the master's gravelly voice rose above the murmur. "This is no day to bow—for today we celebrate. Release our brother."

Lucacius nodded at a hunchbacked wist who stood to his feet, releasing a powerful stench of decaying flesh. Wild eyes staring, the wist waved his decomposing arms about, flinging gobs of rotting flesh from his withered muscles into the excited horde. Amid the cheering and laughter, the wist turned toward the humiliated dragon cowering in his chains.

A certain… fragrance of death, peculiar to the dragon, assailed the nostrils of the faithful as Umbler rose to his feet and stumbled toward his master. There was a sigh of relief among the servants of Dagog as the junior dragon stood. It was not because of pity—for those who serve the beast have none. The horde of hellish monsters were relieved that one among them was given a second chance because they knew, every one of them, that success was not guaranteed. Every assignment had its *possibilities*.

Umbler fell on his face at Dagog's feet, wondering at his release. Dagog reached out his hand and Umbler forgot his broken wings, forgot that his teeth had been crushed by the master in his rage.

"Of course," Umbler conceded "it was my fault. Had I not failed my assignment, the *Seeking* may have sailed past the shores of the Land of Lasciviousness… and there would have been no 'Resisters.' Who can blame Dagog for his rage, considering the damage done to the realm of Darkness by those who no longer drink at his well?" Resisters! Suddenly, Umbler hated the Resisters with a passion that set his belly aflame and ignited fire in his eyes.

Dagog nodded his approval. "Tomorrow," Dagog gloated, "the boy will be mine! Perhaps Umbler's assignment was not, after all, a total failure. So tomorrow—we feast! What do you say?"

The crowd roared its agreement. Always, they agreed with Dagog. And always they were in favor of a feast.

"Tomorrow at sunrise, when the ashes of the deserter rise on the wind—then we celebrate!"

❧

Those who dwell in the Kingdom of Adawm pulled their covers over their ears and complained about the storm that split the heavens. Never were the winds more fierce, the lightning more ferocious than on that dark night.

Dreading the sunrise, Umbler shuffled through the corridors of Darkness with glazed eyes. He had a strange and awful premonition that the celebration was premature.

CHAPTER 22

A Prisoner Set Free

Tears flowed down Brae's battered face, soaking his shirt, transforming the crimson stains on the white fabric to fiery red, fading to palest pink along the edges like a flower freshly bloomed. Regret visited him in his cold cell, sat beside him on the stone floor. Brae put his hands over his face and closed his eyes.

"This is what you chose when you ran away from the Hill of Death at the Cape of Conviction," Regret said.

Tears seeped between Brae's fingers. "I am a liar and a cheat. I deserve to die."

Regret nodded. "You had your chance. You sailed away from the City of Bondage a free man."

Brae looked at the messenger of Truth who sat beside him, his hand resting on Brae's arm. Regret was not an unfriendly sort, but rather comforting. In the present circumstances, Regret seemed to be his only friend, and perhaps his only hope as well.

As if reading Brae's thoughts, Regret said, "I cannot release you from this prison. Your choices have brought you here, and they alone can help you now."

My choices, Brae thought. *I cannot undo what I have already done. I can look back, as Regret has forced me to do, but to go back is impossible.*

"As long as there is life, Brae," Regret said, "choice will be your companion; and every choice you accept will bring with him other choices yet to be accepted or rejected."

As the full moon sailed over the tops of the ancient mamboni trees, a cold wind blew through the bars of his cell. Brae curled into a tight ball and hugged his chest. How he longed to return to the silver birch tree at the Hill of Death, to sit beneath its shade and wrap his arms around its great trunk. He could almost smell the fragrance of the broad leaves, hear the voices of a thousand birds singing in its branches.

Comforted, Brae grew drowsy. Come what may, he would rest in the memory of the silver birch tree. Slumber crept upon him and he felt himself sink down, down, into the dark corridors of the past. A breeze began to stir, refreshing, soothing.

Again, a silver screen unfurled against the blackness. The scene began to unfold: Brae watched his parents cross a bridge to stand upon the deck of a small sailing craft. The name, which had been obscured when Brae saw it before, now glowed softly. It was the *Seeking*! Brae wondered if he was dreaming or awake and seeing into another world. He raised his eyes to the deck of the ship and saw the Messenger facing his parents, his arms outstretched. The couple ran into them and he held them while they cried.

"Did I not promise you that the captives would go free?" he said, and as he spoke the chains fell off the captives and clattered to the deck.

At these words the screen divided, and while Brae watched his mother cry, he could also see the other side.

There was Meriquoi, holding a multitude of people hostage. Some were residents of the City of Bondage. Others Brae recognized as citizens of the Port of Plenty, and some were inhabitants of the Land of Lasciviousness. Yet other hostages he had not met, but they seemed familiar somehow, and he had the strangest feeling that someday he would know them. Many cried out in strange voices, Brae knew he had heard them before, rising from the hold of a ghostly ship.

The screen went dark, but Brae's eyes refused to open. He waited in the darkness, knowing even in his dream that there was more to come.

Suddenly a light a thousand times brighter than the noonday sun shone upon the slave master, capturing Meriquoi in its white-hot beam. The whip in his hand clattered to the floor as wings began to emerge from his back for all to see. Exposed by the light of Truth, the dragon within him sought to escape. The form continued to separate itself from Meriquoi, lifting finally into the air currents to circle the City of Bondage. Smoke billowed from the dragon's mouth, and the birds of the air fled before his rage.

Amazed, Brae stared at Meriquoi. He saw through him, past his flesh and pride and bluster, and found him hollow, haunted, wasted. Somehow, Brae knew that the dragon would return and that Meriquoi would welcome it.

The scene on the silver screen returned to the deck of the *Seeking*. Brae's parents were centered in it, his father holding tightly to his mother's hand as she wept and clung with the other hand to the Messenger.

"But… my baby…" Brae's mother cried over and over; and Brae realized that he was crying with her. "Why can't I take him with me?"

"Each person is called to journey a different route, Miranda, and the way you will go is not the path appointed for the boy."

"But you will come back for him?"

"I will not forget the child," the Messenger promised, "and Immon assures me that his name is inscribed on the palms of His hands. He will not forget."

The *Seeking* departed the shores of the City of Bondage and was soon lost on the horizon. Brae's parents stood at the rail looking back toward the city, their sobs echoing through the night.

The Messenger stood on the dock, watching them go. Brae heard him say, as if to those who were long out of sight, "Any person who has given up houses and lands, brothers and sisters, parents or children for the sake of the King of Kings will receive a hundred times as much and will be received in the Other Kingdom."

The Messenger turned back to the city and Brae lost sight of him. A dove of purest white rose above the trees and circled over the city before settling into the branches of a cocoa palm.

He has always been with me, watching… waiting, Brae thought He sat up and looked around the prison cell. *Something seems.. .different. Maybe it is I who have changed.*

A strong wind rattled the bars of the small window just above Brae's head, and the sound of wings swept the sky, drawing ever nearer the prisoner who hugged his arms across his chest, awaiting the inevitable.

When nothing happened, the silence became unbearable. Brae looked up into the small patch of sky above his head and gasped at the sight of a large white dove perched on the window ledge, pressed against the iron bars. "I will never leave you or forsake you." The words, though unspoken, were clear.

Brae closed his eyes and breathed deeply of the sweet fragrance that blew through the room. The scent of the silver birch tree permeated the cell and brought with it peace like a river—unstoppable, incomprehensible, incomparable peace. Brae gasped as he was swept away, carried back to a place at the foot of the tree. He knew that his body did not move— it was compelled by iron bars and chains to remain in prison. But suddenly he understood how Belita could say that she was free while she served as a slave to Meriquoi. *The body—it is dust and ashes*, Brae thought. *And the spirit that bows before the great King Immon cannot be bound.*

Brae knelt at the foot of the enormous birch tree and pledged his allegiance to the King of Kings who had died to purchase the Certificate of Redemption for a rebellious slave boy in the City of Bondage.

Those who lingered outside the prison to keep watch over the one who would be burned in the fire at sunrise soon found themselves in a deep sleep.

As the pale blush of morning crept across the stone floor, Brae heard a noise above his head and looked up—into the face of the Messenger. He reached up a hand, and the Messenger grasped it. He pulled Brae up, right out of his chains and his cell into the early morning light.

Brae took the Messenger's arm, walking with him between the sleeping villagers' huts. The Messenger helped him into the rowboat. Minutes later, they were on the deck of the *Seeking*.

Brae stood in awkward silence, staring at the deck, reluctant to turn away but at a loss for words.

"Go to bed, Brae," the Messenger said, not unkindly. "Sleep. You will need your strength tomorrow."

Brae slept, and as he did, he dreamt of Belita. Meriquoi stood over her, his whip raised. His muscles rippled beneath a thin shirt; his face twisted in rage. Brae screamed when the whip descended on the helpless woman.

No! Still sleeping, he rolled off his bed onto the floor, striking his head against a post. *Why can't I wake up?* The whip rose and fell with sickening thuds. Belita remained motionless, silent. Blood seeped from a gash on Brae's head and mingled with the blood that flowed down Belita's back.

Brae felt himself drifting, floating on a river of tears. The sun was shining, but it was not hot because a cool breeze stirred the waves. *The current—where is it taking me?*

Belita! She stood on a shore of golden sand, her wounds healed. Then she was walking, running. She stepped into the river and glided swiftly toward the other side. Swathed in white, she glowed like the light, like the sun. Brae shaded his eyes. Reaching the far shore, Belita turned toward him, her beautiful brown eyes smiling at him. Her face was radiant. Lifting a hand, she waved goodbye. Suddenly, she was surrounded by a host of others, all shining like herself, all dressed in white. She reached out and they took her hands.

One stood out from the rest, blinding in his radiance. Belita cried out, "My King!"

The brightness overcame Brae, and he saw no more.

The pastel curtain of a new day draped itself across the sky before Brae opened his eyes. He pulled himself up to sit on his narrow bunk, holding his throbbing head in trembling hands. With a sense of awe, Brae realized that while he slept, the curtains between two worlds had parted, giving him a glimpse into the Other Kingdom.

Brae knew that Belita had died because of him, and he had long carried the bitter weight of guilt. Now it was as if that oppressive burden had dissolved. He had an overwhelming sense that he was forgiven.

Forgiveness is the brother of Freedom. The words came with clarity, not from within his head but from somewhere deeper, clearer. They came from his heart, a heart that had been transformed beneath the branches of the silver birch tree. With Freedom came the courage to remember.

Brae picked up the *Ancient Book of Mysteries* and hugged it against his chest, soaking in the warm glow of the tree embossed on its cover as one soaks in the heat of the sun after a plunge in cold water. Eyes wide open, he sat on his bed, letting the memories of a time long past wash over him like cleansing rain.

So many years ago, a lifetime ago, in the City of Bondage, Belita had taught Brae to believe in the existence of the Other Kingdom, filled his young heart with hopes of freedom. But Brae could not comprehend freedom as Belita knew it, for she believed that it was possible to be free even in the City of Bondage. "When you know the Truth," she used to say, "then you are free."

"How can I be free while Meriquoi is my master?" The words had been bitter in Brae's mouth.

"Real freedom lies within," Belita had said. "No one can take that kind of freedom from you."

Brae had been disgusted. He wanted to be free in his body as well as his mind. Anything less was not freedom, but deception. He had dreamt of escape. He had planned for it. And finally he had tried to achieve it. But the captain of the guard had caught him, pinned him down, and ground his booted foot into Brae's back, waiting for Meriquoi to come and mete out punishment.

Meriquoi had arrived within minutes, flushed with anger and anticipation. He had straddled Brae's body and lifted the whip, but it never lashed the boy's back, for Belita had launched herself across the cobbled road and covered Brae with her own body.

"One life for another!" she had implored. "This youth will bring you much gain on the slave block, Master, while I, a woman past my prime, am nearly useless to you. It is not his fault that he has done this, for I am the one who fueled his desire for freedom. I encouraged him...."

Meriquoi hesitated. "Get up, dog!" he commanded.

Belita had not moved.

The whip descended in fury. It stripped the cloth from Belita's back in one stroke and then found the flesh beneath.

Brae had been paralyzed by fear. This could not be happening. He couldn't speak, couldn't move. Between lashes, Belita had whispered against his ear, "The greatest love in the world is this—" The whip cut into her back. Brae could feel the impact through her body. He cringed. "—to give up your life for a friend." Another lash. A ragged breath. "You are my friend, Brae." Her voice had grown faint; he had to strain to hear. "When you know the Truth—" an awful gasp, like air escaping from a bellows, then faintly "—the Truth will make you free." The breathing stopped.

Meriquoi had tossed the whip to the guard and stomped away. The guard had spat, "Dog!" Then he too turned and walked away, leaving Brae lying on the street, Belita clinging to his back even in death.

Brae had stumbled to his feet. Gathering the broken body into his arms, he carried Belita outside the city gates and buried her. Stacking stones over the freshly turned dirt, he had written a memorial for the only person who had ever loved him: here lies Belita. she died free. A week later, the Messenger had come to the City of Bondage.

His tears spent, Brae curled up on the bunk and slept. Peace coursed through his battered soul like a life-giving stream; forgiveness freely given was at last received.

CHAPTER 23

The End of Umbler

U mbler saw the master coming. There was no place to hide, no escape. He fell on the ground and covered his face with a broken wing. The thunder of heavy steps drew near. Umbler could not breathe. He peeked out from beneath his wing and fainted dead away. Dagog, followed by Lucacius, advanced, murder in his eyes. There would be no second chances.

I should have known was the last thought Umbler remembered.

And it would have been his last thought, except for his amazing luck. At the last moment, a spear of lightening zapped through the sky; white-hot flames seared the heavens, singeing hide and fur alike.

A faint stream of light pierced the haze and Umbler felt himself rousing from the pitch-black realm of unconsciousness. *So the scream I heard was not my own*, the dragon marveled, his callused hands exploring his wings, his scaly body, his beaked face—all his body parts seemed intact. *It must have been Dagog.* Umbler wished he could have seen him, a fallen star plunging from the middle clouds.

If a dragon could smile, Umbler might have, but he was already scheming his way back into Dagog's goodwill. *There is a little island that is mostly uninhabited to the south*, he thought, careful to protect his broken wing as he headed in that direction.

I have a little time. Dagog will not be doling out any kicks until his own bottom recovers. If a dragon could be thankful, Umbler would have been grateful to whomever it may have been that was big enough to kick his master out of the sky.

CHAPTER 24

Crashed on the Rocks

E arly one morning, the Messenger told Brae to turn the ship out of the open sea and follow a course that seemed unfamiliar. He turned the ship into a narrow channel between the cliffs of the mainland and a series of rocky islands. Brae watched. laughing, as the wind filled the sails. The years had added lines to his face and hair to his chin, but they had failed to dull his excitement with his journey. He could hardly wait to explore the new lands they were now approaching.

Above the sound of the waves that slapped the sides of the ship, Brae heard what sounded like a feeble cry for help. With it came another sound that brought fear to his heart, a distant roar that grew louder each moment as the wind drove the *Seeking* farther along the channel. The tide roared through the ever-narrowing waterway, churning into whirlpools and smashing against the cliffs on both sides. A milky mist rose from the cascade of rushing water. Silently, Brae turned to the Messenger. Had the time come for him to die?

"We must go on, Brae, not to die but to rescue the dying. Listen! There is a sound louder than the wind and stronger than the water. Listen with your heart, and you will know why you have been drawn to this place."

Peering into the billowing mist, Brae could see a vision—the sad faces of men, women, and children who were lost and struggling to stay afloat on the Sea of Life, crying out in fear and sorrow.

Tears filled Brae's eyes. He said to the Messenger, "Please send me to help them."

Looking out over the white-capped water, Brae saw the splintered boards and floating debris of a broken ship. Then he saw a man in the water. He threw out a lifeline and drew the man to safety.

The cold, wet stranger stood shivering before Brae, rivulets of icy water drizzling from his short-cropped hair, trickling down his face, and glistening like diamonds on his salt-and-pepper beard.

He grasped Brae's hand. "Thank you," he gasped, "for… saving my life."

With that, the man collapsed onto the deck. Brae half carried, half dragged the man below deck, put him to bed in one of the bunks, and piled blankets over him. Then he prepared a bowl of hot soup.

"When you have rested," Brae said, "I would like to hear your story."

Back on deck, Brae stood long at the rail, listening for the sounds rising from the sea. A cacophony of voices filled the night—birds calling to their mates, lions commanding their prides, and wolves howling at the moon. But these were harmonious voices, not those of people lost on the

Sea of Life. The voices of the lost were silent. Brae retired to his bed. Perhaps tomorrow they would speak again, and he would sail forward to find them, bring them aboard the ship, and invite them to join him on the journey to the Other Kingdom.

Brae rose with the sun. Following his nose to the galley, he found breakfast on the table. The stranger, who was already seated, nodded and poured a second cup of coffee. Over a steaming bowl of oatmeal and dried fruit, he told his story.

"My name," he began, "is Mikhail. I was sailing peacefully on the Sea of Life when I heard cries for help. I was drawn by the wind into the rushing channel. Once there, I found I could not get out. I was powerless against the forces of wind and water. My ship, *Good Works*, stuck fast on a rock and was smashed to pieces. I survived by clinging to the rock until you arrived."

"Where were you bound when you were distracted by the voices?" Brae asked.

"I seek the Other Kingdom," Mikhail answered, drawing a deep breath. "I was born in the City of Self-reliance. I had a happy childhood there. But one day, someone I loved very much became ill, and there was nothing I could do to help. When she died, I left the city and began seeking something greater than myself. I discovered it in a place called the Cape of Conviction. Since that day, I have followed the great King Immon, who took my place on the Hill of Death."

"I have been there," Brae said solemnly. With these four words a friendship was forged that would not be easily sundered, born of a common experience and a shared vision, a quest for the Other Kingdom.

After a long silence made comfortable by their bond, Brae asked, "Have you met the Messenger?"

Mikhail nodded. "It was he who stayed with me in the churning currents of the channel, holding my head above water until you arrived."

"I sail with him," Brae said. "We would be honored if you would join us in our journey."

Mikhail nodded, too moved to speak.

CHAPTER 25
Mikhail's Story

Mikhail pushed away from the table and climbed the narrow stairs. He stood on the sun-bleached deck with tears misting his eyes. When his ship hit the rock, Mikhail had believed his journey to be over, his quest a failure. His beautiful ship *Good Works* had been destroyed, its rich wood splintered, its sails torn. *Good Works* could never take him to the Other Kingdom.

He had wanted to give up, to sink beneath the swirling water, and allow the current to drag him along the rocks until his body was as broken as his ship. But he had not given up because he had not been alone in the water; somewhere deep inside of him a flame still burned—a flame that had been ignited long ago beneath the spreading branches of the silver birch tree.

Mikhail leaned against the rail, remembering. Anastasia had just died. He had wanted to die with her. In that dark hour, life had no meaning, no purpose without her. She had been the light of his life, his anchor, his beacon. She had been everything to him.

They had grown up together in the City of Self-reliance, married, and begun a successful career together as merchants. They had traveled the world, built a lucrative business, visited exotic places, and met people of wealth and stature. And they had not forgotten the poor. Mikhail and Anastasia were well known for their contributions to the needy.

Then Anastasia had become ill. Mikhail had taken her to the best doctors and bought the latest medicines. Still, a hacking cough from deep within had racked her body, draining her strength and robbing her of breath. Day by day she had grown weaker, more fragile. Helplessly, Mikhail had watched his beloved fade away.

The day after her body had been committed to the earth, Mikhail boarded his ship and headed out to sea. He did not know where he was going. He did not care. Life in the City of Self-reliance had ended for him. He would never go back.

That was how he came to disembark at the Cape of Conviction his life in ruins, his fortune meaningless, his heart ripped apart.

What had drawn him to the dreary shores of the Cape of Conviction? Mikhail knew that it was the grayness of the place—the melancholic whine of the wind through the tall white stones rising in quiet dignity against the sky. Surely they meant something! There was significance here. And he was desperate to discover anything of importance to restore meaning to his empty life.

He stumbled ashore, believing the city to be deserted. He was taken by surprise when the vigilantes who swarmed from the Department of Justice building arrested him. He didn't resist, but walked meekly past the bronze statue into the courtroom where he would be tried for crimes he didn't understand.

From his high-backed chair behind a polished mahogany bench, the black-robed judge looked at Mikhail in somber disapproval.

"Do you know the crimes that have been recorded against you?" he asked, frowning over his spectacles.

"No," Mikhail answered. "I have been a good man, a faithful husband, and an honorable citizen, dwelling most of my life in the City of Self-reliance. I have given much of my wealth to help the poor and have broken no laws. I do not understand why I have been arrested."

The judge nodded, then motioned to the bailiff at his right hand. "Andrae," he commanded, "start the scene."

A mist arose from the floor; it covered one wall, and in it an image began to appear: a desert town that Mikhail recognized from long ago. A man stood before a hostile crowd. He basked in a serenity that seemed out of place as a mob of men shook their fists in his face, writhing like snakes in their rage. They bound him, beat him, and left him for dead, and still that sense of tranquility covered him like a garment.

Mikhail saw himself standing in the crowd, looking on with disinterest. "How could I stand there doing nothing?" He wanted to look away, but the scene was not over.

He saw a man from the mob approach him. Mikhail knew this man, a merchant, and didn't like him, knew that he traded in humanity, sold men, women, and children into slavery. Yet Mikhail traded with the man, bought his silk and spices, carved figurines and ivory trinkets.

The scene shifted, and Mikhail's face flushed with shame, for there he was, eating at this man's table, ignoring his bloody hands. Mikhail trembled as he watched himself take out his bag and pass gold coins to the merchant. He could watch no more.

Mikhail pled guilty to all the charges against him. He expected no less than death for his crimes. He welcomed it, for death would end his useless existence, quiet the ache in his broken heart. He could ask no more.

The judge rose, lifting his robe with age-spotted hands to avoid the dust that puffed around his feet with each step. He escorted Mikhail from the courtroom, leading him along a path that wound up a gentle incline to the cemetery he had seen from the ship. On the peak of the hill stood an enormous silver birch tree. Its branches soared above the mist that draped itself like a sodden blanket over the Hill of Death to embrace the clouds beyond. Crickets chirped and birds sang their melancholy songs as the judge retreated down the hill, leaving Mikhail alone in the shadow of the ancient tree.

As he sat there, his back against its mammoth trunk, Mikhail soon became aware that he was not alone. Someone sat beside him, resting against the tree. Mikhail was not startled. It was as if this one had been there all along.

Mikhail closed his eyes. He was so tired. He did not sleep, but he rested, perfectly at peace in the presence of one he did not know, on the Hill of Death. After a while—minutes, hours, Mikhail did not know, for time had ceased to exist for him, sitting there among the graves—he looked into the eyes of the one beside him. It was as if he fell into them. He felt himself swimming in deep pools of mystery, and peace rushed through him. He could not move, did not want to. As the river of peace rushed in, all the agony, sorrow, and despair flowed out of him.

Broken and mended, weak and wiser, Mikhail tried to rise. He fell to his knees. His head bowed, he waited. The one beside him stood and placed a hand upon Mikhail's head. Strength—power such as he had never known—coursed through his body. *He restores my soul.* Where had those words come from? They were unspoken, yet they echoed in the depths of his being: *He restores my soul.*

Mikhail stood. He was alone. And yet he knew somehow that he would never be alone again.

He returned to his ship, *Good Works*, and resumed his journey. It was then that he had crashed upon the rocks.

As he stood at the rail, Mikhail knew that he didn't need the broken ship; he needed only the one who stood beside him, as he continued his journey on the Sea of Life.

CHAPTER 26

The City of
Broken Dreams

T he sun bore down, and a gentle breeze billowed the sails of the *Seeking*. Above the song of the wind whistling through the rigging, voices could once again be heard. "Help me," they wailed. But this time the voices came not from the sea but from the land. On the shore ahead, Brae could see the lights of a city set upon a hill. As they drew near, the voices grew louder.

"We must stop here!" Brae dropped the anchor. When he and Mikhail went ashore, the voices ceased. Everyone in the city seemed to be in a hurry, too busy to pay any attention to the two strangers who had come among them. Everyone except one man. He sat on a bench in a crowded park while children laughed and played around him. His clothing was tattered, his beard unkempt. He looked as if he had not slept in a long time. He looked up through squinted eyes when Brae and Mikhail approached.

"What do you want?" the man asked, slouching deeper into his oversized coat.

"What do *you* want is the question," Mikhail answered, smiling.

"No one cares what I want," the man scoffed, his hands fumbling in his pockets. "Why should they? I am nobody!"

"Do you have a name?"

"I am called Odair, but I am still nobody."

"You don't have to be." Brae was near his face now. "Come, join Mikhail and me in our quest for the Other Kingdom."

"I don't know of any... Other Kingdom." Odair lifted his hand as if to brush off an annoying insect, then looked away.

"But do you not dream of a place where men walk together in harmony?" Brae asked. "Of a life that is mingled with the lives of others, no man walking alone?" Excited, Brae grabbed Odair's shoulders and turned him around to face him. "Don't you want to fight the good fight, slay dragons in the name of the great King Immon? Don't you want your life to mean something before it is over and you stand empty-handed before the great King with nothing to offer in return for the breath that he gave you these many years?"

Odair leapt to his feet. "Stop!" he shouted, alarming the children nearby and sending them scooting off to play in another corner of the park. "You speak of that which once I dreamed of. It is too late for me! I have lived a lifetime in this city of empty promises and broken dreams. I wasted my youth and am ready to end this useless existence."

He pulled his hand from his pocket. In it was a small packet. "This is the day I die! I have no spirit left in my breast to compel me to this quest. I am a wasted man." With these words, Odair opened the packet and poured its contents into a cup of water beside him on the bench.

As he raised the cup to his lips, Brae knocked it from his hand with a swift motion. Brae and Mikhail knelt before the man. "You must believe in that which you cannot see," Brae urged gently. "There is a Kingdom far greater than the Kingdom of Adawm. If you could only know the price that was paid so that you could enter there, you would go with us and claim your inheritance."

Hope, like the tiny flame of a single candle, ignited in the heart of the despairing man. He rose uncertainly to his feet.

"Do something!" Dagog screamed to no one in particular. We are losing another one!"

Lucacius sat on his haunches. He knew what was coming and wanted no part of it. He was not going to risk incurring the wrath of Immon by interfering with the drama unfolding in the City of Broken Dreams. Not today. He had seen this scene before, and was in no mood to challenge the servants of Immon.

"Go!" Dagog commanded. "Tear those two impostors apart! Go get 'em, Lucacius! What are you doing slinking away from me? I am your master! Do you hear me?"

Lucacius melted into the shadows and was gone, leaving Dagog fuming in impotent fury. Lucacius was evil, but he wasn't ignorant. He had managed to avoid destruction at the hands of Immon for many years by knowing when to hide and when to go for the kill. This was a time to hide. It seemed

Lucacius had been doing a lot of hiding lately. He didn't like it.

∾

Immon sat on his throne beside the emperor watching the scene unfold in the City of Broken Dreams. They laughed as Lucacius did his disappearing act and Dagog, like a rabid beast, chased after him. They laughed again, this time with joy, as Odair, standing unsteadily, reached out his hand to grasp Brae's arm and committed himself to the quest for the Other King-dom.

∾

Unseen by the eyes of flesh, a huge whelter, long and fat, lost its hold on the former servant of Dagog and fell, screeching, to the ground.

Whelters were one of Dagog's favorite weapons in the battle for the souls of mankind. They were slimy wraithlike creatures who would wrap themselves around the throat of an unsuspecting person and slowly suck the blood. This they replaced with vile green poison that numbed the senses and caused the victim to lose his focus. Without it, he might wander the Kingdom of Adawm for his entire life, unaware that he had missed out on the quest for the Other Kingdom and had lost his inheritance—until he stood before Immon with empty hands, realizing too late the loss of his treasure.

∾

The sun was setting over the Sea of Life when the three travelers reached the ship. The Messenger stood, waiting. He reached out a hand and pulled Odair onto the deck.

In the days that followed, the *Seeking* sailed once more. Having known the misery of those wandering in darkness, Odair wanted to stop at every port along the way and tell his story. Some who heard it joined the quest for the Other Kingdom. Many walked away in sadness, unwilling to accept so costly a gift. Others drove the servants of Immon from their shores and clung to the darkness that consumed them.

Odair stood often at the rail of the ship, gazing across the waves, watching for the next port while Brae and Mikhail took turns at the wheel. Tiring days and sleepless nights were a small price to pay for the privilege of rescuing those lost at sea. The Messenger moved among them, encouraging, strengthening, and guiding them in their quest. Always, the shadow of Dagog hovered over the *Seeking*, but those who traveled in the company of the Messenger took little notice.

CHAPTER 27

Umbler's Return

L ucacius sat back on his haunches, his head cocked, watching the dragon's approach. "What happened to you?" the wolven said. "You look like you just crawled out of the pit."

Umbler raised his gnarled fist and Lucacius felt the wiry hair on his back grow rigid. The wolven stared at the long talons, ebony razors that looked as if they could slash his nose right off his face. Lucacius wondered if Umbler had forgotten the wart incident.

"No," Umbler said, accurately interpreting the wolven's anxiety. "I do not forget."

Lucacius stood and began to circle the dragon. Umbler fixed his stare on a distant star and refused to look at the wolven.

"You have grown… bigger," Lucacius said. "Stronger." The bulging muscles beneath the dragon's wings were impressive.

Returning to his haunches, he faced the dragon. "You have been… busy?"

"How long has it been," Umbler's voice was low, restrained, "since you visited the island city of Decarpia?"

Lucacius stared at Umbler, forgetting to close his mouth. "Decarpia?"

Umbler sniffed. The fragrance of fear. He breathed deeply—as he had done often in Decarpia. He had learned to thrive on fear in the past twelve months. Fear and hatred, rage and death. He took great satisfaction in the grudging admiration of his general.

"It is… your domain, I believe?" An unpleasant smile spread across the dragon's scarred face. "Dagog will not be pleased to know of your… neglect."

"You don't dare approach the master," Lucacius growled. "He thinks you have been retired to the pit."

"Would you like to tell him that you failed to locate me?" Umbler asked.

"What do you—"

"Want?" Umbler finished the wolven's sentence. "I want a new name. By that name I will become great and none will remember the shame of my earlier… failure."

"How are you known—"

"In Decarpia?" Umbler finished for the wolven. "I am known as Asama of Decarpia."

"An impressive title." The general nodded. "It shall be yours. But first I must visit Decarpia."

"And you will be certain to inform Dagog that his subject, Asama, has cast his spell over the city of Decarpia."

"I will tell him when I have seen it." Lucacius turned and sprinted for the city, hoping that Asama was a braggart and a liar.

CHAPTER 28

A Daring Rescue

T he Sea of Life flowed along the shores of the Kingdom of Adawm, where many people were born and died without ever really living at all. Not knowing the route to the Other Kingdom, Brae and Mikhail followed the Messenger's directions, now sailing on boldly, at other times appearing to backtrack. Brae was not entirely surprised, therefore, when one day a familiar landscape appeared on the horizon—the Land of Lasciviousness.

At sunset, Brae and Mikhail went ashore, leaving Odair on board to guard the *Seeking*.

Brae stood once more before the huge bonfire, watching the naked dancers leap through the flames. He shook his head at the thought of how he had failed when he had last stood before this fire. How many seasons had passed since that day? The boy who had danced before the fire had long since yielded to maturity—to years spent in the company of the Messenger. The boy had come to the Land of Lasciviousness in ignorance, seeking excitement. The man came in obedience, seeking to set other captives free.

Seeing Brae and Mikhail, the dancers urged, "Come, dance with us. We pay homage to the god of the night. He will be displeased if you do not join us."

"We pay homage to the great King Immon," Brae answered.

"Who is this... Immon?" a young man asked.

"He is King of Kings and rightful Ruler over all the kingdoms of the world." Brae replied.

"He is no king here," a young woman said. "We serve no king but the Prince of the Darkness, whose beneficence we all enjoy."

"All true goodness comes from the hand of the King whom you reject," Mikhail said. "Dagog, whom you call Prince of the Darkness, claims a false honor. It is not Dagog who sends the rain upon your fields and gives fertility to your livestock. It is the great King Immon who loves you and requires your allegiance—if you would not see death in this land."

"What do you mean?" the woman asked, startled. "Would the king of whom you speak war against us?"

"It is the Prince of the Darkness who has poisoned your wells and blinded your eyes," Brae said. "Life and peace can be found in none other than the great King Immon.

"I am weary of all this talk," the woman said. "Pay homage to your king and to our prince as well."

"The Prince of the Darkness, whom you honor, is an enemy to our king,"

Mikhail answered. "We have no desire to honor him.

The woman spat on the ground. "Then be gone! If you will not dance before the god of the night, our prince will be angry because of you."

Suddenly, the Land of Lasciviousness was in an uproar. An old man picked up a club and leapt at Brae, swinging the weapon with surprising strength. Brae held up his hands to deflect the blows. Mikhail was warding off blows as well, as other villagers picked up sticks and clubs and joined the fray. Children threw stones at them as they fled for their lives. They outran the angry crowd, jumped into their boat, and began rowing toward the *Seeking*.

"Wait! Please…!"

Several yards down the shore a woman stood huddled with three small children.

"Take us with you," she called. "We will not live if you leave us here!"

Brae looked at Mikhail. Was this a trick? Already the angry dancers, brandishing clubs and stones, had noticed the woman and had turned toward her. The children were silent, clinging to her, terror scrunching their small faces.

"Let's go back!" Brae shouted.

Angry voices roared into a firestorm of rage as the villagers began running toward the helpless mother and children. Raising their clubs, they howled like beasts of prey.

Desperately, the woman stepped into the water and waded toward the boat, carrying one child on her shoulders and one in each arm. Brae reached out and pulled her and the children into the boat just as the first stone was thrown. The jagged rock glanced off her shoulder before thudding into the bottom of the boat. She did not cry out, but quickly pushed the children onto the floor and covered them with her body. Stones and heavy sticks rained down upon the boat, bruising, drawing blood.

It seemed to Brae that the young men of the land would surely overtake the small rowboat. Just as he was about to despair, a lion sprang out of the forest, an immense beast, muscles rippling beneath a blur of tawny fur and golden mane. He leapt into the angry mob, roaring, slashing, and biting. It seemed as if the whole land shook, and the trees bent low before a strong wind, like subjects bowing before a king. Stones thudded to the ground as villagers dropped them like burning coals and ran for their lives. The young men, seeing the fate of their companions, turned toward a distant shore where they emerged from the water moments later and made for their village.

Shaken, but full of joy, Brae and Mikhail returned to the *Seeking*. They were welcomed by the Messenger, who wrapped the woman and her children in woolen blankets and brought them hot tea. When they were warm and comfortable, the Messenger sent them below deck to sleep.

They would need their rest, for in a few hours another battle would begin.

CHAPTER 29

An Old Friend

T he woman stood at the rail of the *Seeking*, her slender form bent backward like a willow before the wind. Her upturned face was bathed in the reflected glory of a thousand shining lights, sparkling in the night sky like tiny suns. She stood without moving, absorbing the wind, the sky, the sea, and the solitude. Wrapped in tranquillity as in a blanket, she breathed in the quiet. As in the calm before a storm, the sea seemed subdued.

The Messenger approached quietly, not wanting to startle her. "Salina." He reached out to touch her arm.

She turned to look into his face without surprise. Smiling, Salina took his hand.

"I know you," she said. "You came to my village when I was a child. Miarrow and Miammi sat around the fire with you when Sodomon was chief. Though Sodomon rejected you, my parents believed in you and remained loyal to Immon."

From a bag slung over her shoulder she took a brown leather journal. Its cover was torn and stained, its pages worn from much use. Her eyes misted over.

"Miarrow made this for me, and Miammi sewed the pages into the binding. They said I should write an account of the suffering in the Land of Lasciviousness so that I would never forget the example of those who chose to suffer for Immon rather than remain in bondage to the Prince of the Darkness. I have written all that happened after you left."

She handed the journal to the Messenger.

"Sometime," she said, "I would like you to read it. For now, please tell me, are my children safe aboard this ship?"

"They are under the protection of the great King Immon, Salina," the Messenger said, placing the worn journal back in her hand. "Go and sleep now. You will need your rest tomorrow."

As Salina gazed into the Messenger's eyes, peace settled on her shoulders like a garment. She returned to her children, who slumbered in a tiny bunk tucked into a corner of the galley. She pulled a blanket over herself and her three little ones and soon fell asleep.

Salina arose with the sun and slipped up the stairs to find the Messenger standing at the wheel, staring at something in the distance. Following his gaze, Salina studied the horizon. The *Seeking* was drifting with the wind toward a shallow bay. Just beyond the beach, the tops of mighty trees swayed in the morning breeze. Birds of paradise darted among the leaves, making their presence known with shrill calls.

The Messenger turned to Salina. "Do you see the dragon ship?"

Salina looked over her shoulder. Far out to sea, on the edge of the horizon, was a dark smudge of cloud. She nodded.

"There will be war. Tonight. We must get you and the children off the ship. I have prepared a place for you among the Newah. They are a gentle people and kind, but they do not know the way to the Other Kingdom. Go to them. They will treat you well, and in return you will open their eyes. Do you see the smoke that rises on yonder mountain? It is the morning fires of the Newah village. You must go now."

Salina's children crowded around her, grabbing her hand, clutching her dress. She pointed to the boat that waited, bobbing on the swells.

She helped each child over the rail and into the rowboat. "We are going up that mountain." She pointed to a white-capped peak that rose out of the morning mist. Seeing the bag of food in the bottom of the boat, she smiled. "We are going to find the Newah village, and they are going to love you—just as I do!" The children snuggled close to Salina as she settled in beside them and the Messenger took the oars.

The Messenger rowed the boat the short distance to shore and helped the children make their way onto the powdery white sand. Salina accepted the hand the Messenger extended and stepped lightly out of the boat. He handed her the bag of food. When she turned to say goodbye, the Messenger wrapped her in his strong arms and held her for a moment, infusing her with his strength, his courage, and his love. Then he released her and stepped into the boat.

Salina sang as she led her children into the forest. Even as she watched him row toward the ship, she had a sense that the Messenger was still as close as the air she breathed. She would only have to call his name and he would be there. She knew that she would never be alone again.

∽

The Messenger pulled hard at the oars as he returned to the good ship *Seeking*, thinking of the surprise that awaited Salina in the Newah village. *You will soon see, my little one*, he thought, remembering an entry he had noted as he had turned the pages of Salina's journal, *that happiness is possible at times, even for those who do not possess the innocence of children.*

Peering into the waning mists of morning, the Messenger saw that the rescue of Salina had not gone unnoticed. Sulfuric fumes boiled out of the dragon ship, polluting the earth, sea, and sky with the stench of death. Little wonder that the flagstaff of the dreadful vessel was a dragon with bloody hands and fiery eyes.

"I have come to steal, to kill, and to destroy," Dagog had boasted countless times in centuries past. So he said when cities burned and the blood of innocents ran thick in the streets.

"Your definition of death is as twisted as your knotted skull," the Messenger said aloud, knowing that Dagog had spies everywhere.

Low-pitched chanting aboard the dragon ship, interrupted by the occasional shriek of an agonized soul, floated over the water. It was the sound of terror, of pain, of evil. The Messenger longed to clap his hands over his ears to shut out the repugnant noise, but he held steady at the oars, for he knew that the battle was at hand.

As the Messenger climbed aboard the ship, he saw a small group of warriors gathered on the deck. They were aware of the threat that rode the seas, but he knew they would not have called themselves warriors. They had no knowledge of the power that rested upon them.

The evening passed, and the dragon ship launched no attack. The weary warriors huddled, waiting. Fatigue, excitement, and apprehension eroded their strength, and they slept.

One among them returned, in his dreams it seemed, to a place across the great sea. Seven or eight years old he may have been. And there he sat beside Belita, his arms locked around her ample waist, his hair sticking up in all directions. His eyes shone with unshed tears and yet were full of wonder.

"What is the Other Kingdom like?" the boy asked.

"Oh," Belita said, "it is a magical place, like a Kingdom of castles and everyone who lives there gets adopted by the great King Immon. Imagine, Brae, a kingdom of royalty. Why, you would be a prince!"

Long after midnight, dark forms began to move about the dragon ship. The *Avenger* weighed anchor and began to converge on the *Seeking*. Under cover of darkness, the forces of Dagog came, burning in their quest for blood.

CHAPTER 30

The Standoff

Dagog was not deceived by Umbler's new identity, but after viewing the death and devastation wrought by the dragon in the city of Decarpia, he promoted Asama to second in command under the authority of Lucacius.

"The boy is mine." Asama returned the wolven's glare with his own.

"He is no longer a boy," Lucacius growled. "Do you think you are—"

"Strong enough?" Asama finished. He lifted his mammoth wings, and the intoxicating scent of sulfur intensified aboard the Avenger. He opened his mouth wide revealing four rows of razor-sharp teeth and exhaled a black cloud of acidic breath. "Do you contest my power?"

The wolven took a step backward and crouched low, a deep growl rumbling from his massive throat.

Dagog leaned against the iron rail that wound along the port side of the *Avenger*. *Interesting*, he thought. *Lucacius has a challenger*. Dagog was tiring of Lucacius. *Dragon blood will soon flow*, he predicted.

But for now, there was an enemy to conquer. "Stop it!" he roared, and the wolven and the dragon fell back, forgetting their quarrel. "It is time. Go and destroy the deserters aboard the *Seeking*."

CHAPTER 31

The Shadow of Death

T he Messenger nudged Brae. "Wake up!" he shouted. "The enemy is upon you!"

In a rush they came, forms without substance, darting like bats through the deepening darkness, slithering like serpents over the rail.

Never had the good ship *Seeking* hosted such fearsome and grotesque creatures, for Dagog coveted this prize, this trophy of Immon. His call for reinforcements had sounded long ago, and thousands of creatures that served the Prince of the Darkness had rendezvoused aboard the dragon ship, awaiting this hour.

∾

The Messenger recognized Lucacius. He remembered the dark ceremony in the shadowed wood of the Valley of E'ure where Lucacius had been commissioned general over Dagog's forces.

"You have to catch them before they discover the tree," Dagog had instructed Lucacius, "for it is very difficult to trip them up afterward."

"How do they discover it?" Lucacius had asked.

"The silver birch tree is musical, though most do not know it," Dagog had said. "The symphony played upon its branches sings always throughout the Kingdom of Adawm. If any subject of the kingdom hesitates, even for a moment, in his quest to please himself, he may hear the music and fall into its embrace, never to be the same again."

"What should I do if one should discover the tree," Lucacius said, "and be offended by it?"

"That one," Dagog had said with a sly grin, "is ripe for the picking."

Bloodsuckers like the one that had attached itself to Odair swarmed across the gleaming deck of the *Seeking*, leaving trails of slime in their wake. Less numerous but more deadly were the whelters. These were the fast-acting "rattler" species. Their bodies were forest green with yellow diamond shapes on their backs. Their bite was painful, their venom deadly. Within minutes of attaching themselves to a victim, they infused the bloodstream with enough poison to deteriorate the muscles of the heart and shut down the nervous system. The whelters were vicious, ruthless creatures.

There were also the wists, ancient inhabitants of the Kingdom of Adawm. Once creatures of flesh, they were now translucent, like milky shadows, floating stealthily over the surface of the earth or water. Reeking of death, intent on plunder, shrieking and howling, they leapt upon their prey, the toxic stench of their breath sickening all who came near.

Lucacius and others of his kind, whelters, wists, and myriad other deformed and demented creatures, wild with bloodlust, now crowded aboard the *Seeking*. The servants of Immon found breathing difficult in the presence of such odorous creatures.

Brae was the first to raise his sword. He was unafraid. He knew the power of the weapon in his hand. He remembered the day it had been given to him.

He was barely seventeen, and his journey had only begun. He had just had his first glimpse of the beast, Dagog, and longed to turn back to the City of Bondage. Had it not been for his fear that Meriquoi would kill him, he would have.

It was then that the Messenger had commanded him to kneel on the deck of the *Seeking*. The Messenger had taken his own sword from the sheath that hung at his side and raised it high. Brae remembered the glint of the sun on the blade and the ruby handle radiating streams of blood-red light as the Messenger held it aloft. He touched Brae's shoulders, first the right, then the left, and handed the sword to Brae.

Brae had looked at it, uncomprehending. Never had anyone given him a gift. And this was no ordinary sword. Brae could tell by the light that shone from within the honed steel.

"What do I do with this?" he had whispered.

"You will know what to do when the time comes," the Messenger answered, and Brae had known that no matter what happened in the journey on the Sea of Life, all would be well in the end.

The time to use the sword had come! Brae knew no fear as he wielded the weapon given to him so long ago. Evil creatures leapt at him in the darkness and were swiftly felled by the sharp blade. Brae fought bravely as the dark clouds swirled overhead.

The night was long. The servants of Immon grew weary—yet they resisted the onslaught of Dagog. They would not yield to the Prince of the Darkness.

∽

Addar stood before his throne, consulting with two generals, his eyes fixed on the drama unfolding on the great stage of life in the Kingdom of Adawm. He glanced at Immon who, unseen, secretly directed the battle. He smiled. His son commanded the mighty warriors of the Other Kingdom with confidence and power. The throne room was bursting with messengers from the battlefield. The hoard of warriors in service to Dagog had grown throughout the night. Reinforcements streamed from the dragon ship. For every dark warrior that fell, another arrived to take his place.

A legion of shining ones stood at attention. Why did Addar delay intervention? Though some may have wondered, none questioned the emperor, for ancient history had proven his wisdom.

Another room in the palace bustled with activity. It was the magnificent banquet hall of the king. Mahogany tables arranged end to end stretched as far as the eye could see. Crystal dishes were laden with food that tantalized the senses. Though all of the food was grown in the Other Kingdom, there were vegetarian dishes that looked and smelled like beef, fish, and chicken. Other plates held steaming vegetables saturated in creamy butter. There were sweet breads and garlic breads, white breads and rye breads. Tall goblets of crimson juices alternated with clear sparkling juices.

In the center of each table was an enormous vase of fresh flowers in many shapes and colors. Each emitted a heady sweet perfume, and music flowed from every petal, blending into a harmonious symphony of joy.

A banner flew high above the place of honor. It read Welcome Home, Brae, Servant of The Great King. Everywhere there was a sense of excitement, of anticipation, like the night before Christmas when the tree is surrounded by presents.

The Messenger appeared at the throne, head bowed, listening intently.

Immon spoke. "It is time," he said, "to bring our servant home." He settled on his throne. Soon his beloved servant would arrive. He could hardly wait to embrace him, to say to him before all the citizens of the Other Kingdom, "You have done well and proven yourself a good and faithful servant."

The Messenger nodded, then stepped back into the realm of the Kingdom of Adawm.

The Messenger stood beside Brae. He loved the celebration of homecoming, but dreaded the process. There was always pain, always sorrow, for those left behind.

Brae's sword flashed through the air, decapitating a sleek whelter that had launched itself at him from the mast. He whirled, catching one of Lucacius' kind under the chin just before its fangs buried themselves in his neck. Brae twisted back around, his sword reaching for the wist that had thrust a blood-encrusted dagger at his heart. Brae's sword found its mark, but not before the dagger ripped through his shirt, finding the soft flesh beneath, puncturing his lung.

The Messenger flinched, feeling the pain of Brae's wound in his own side. A crimson stain spread across Brae's chest. He looked surprised but did not fall. Holding one hand over his heart, he continued to fight with the other, though he felt his strength flowing out of him.

❧

In the throne room, Immon rose to his feet. "It is enough!" he shouted, releasing a legion of shining warriors to enter the battle. Like comets, the warriors streaked through the night sky. Dark warriors fell like rain before them.

A whelter had wrapped its wraithlike body around Mikhail's neck and was about to sink its fangs into the jugular. Within seconds, deadly poison would enter his bloodstream. Still he fought, not granting even so much as a glance to the slimy creature. A shining warrior flicked the whelter with the end of his sword, dumping it, shrieking and writhing, into the water, where vile poison emptied out of him and dispersed into the depths of the sea.

Aboard the dragon ship, Dagog shouted, "Fire the cannon!"

As the order was obeyed, one of Immon's warriors reached out his hand and caught the fiery ball, flinging it back upon the dragon ship.

There was a tremendous explosion. The waters leapt high into the sky as if to douse the stars. The dragon ship splintered into a thousand pieces and disappeared. All grew calm. The great noise and light of the blast subsided, and the fingers of dawn spread across the horizon. In the transition, an immense dark shadow left the shattered dragon ship and returned to the region of the air that was its domain.

The servants of Immon were exhausted, but victorious. The Shadow of Death was behind them. Before them, sparkling like diamonds in the morning sun, was a ribbon of crystal.

"The Crystal River," murmured the Messenger.

Well done, my good and faithful servant.

CHAPTER 32
The Crossing

T he Crystal River flowed along the edge of the Sea of Life bordering the Other Kingdom. Its shores were lined with golden avenues. Trees grew in profusion along the fertile banks, sinuous branches stretched toward the cloudless sky, fragrant fruit dripping from their fingers. The travelers were so enchanted by the Crystal River and the land beyond it that no one noticed Brae, slumped on the deck of the *Seeking*. The Messenger knelt beside him.

"You are wounded," the Messenger said.

"It is… over." Brae coughed as he struggled to speak. Blood covered his shirt under the blanket wrapped tightly around him.

Mikhail rushed to his side. "Oh, Messenger, save him!" Mikhail pleaded.

The Messenger touched Brae's shoulder. Tears glistened in his eyes. "It is finished," he said.

Brae felt strength flow through him at the touch of the Messenger's hand. He stood to his feet. Suddenly, he felt as light as air. He stepped over the rail into the cool waters of the Crystal River. That was when he first glimpsed the land on the other side and recognized it as the Other Kingdom. "I made it!" He laughed and cried and tried to wade faster though the water to get to the other side.

A crowd stood at the water's edge, clapping and cheering, urging Brae on. A dark-skinned woman with long ebony hair, clothed in a white robe that shone like the noonday sun, raced through the crowd. Belita! Brae reached out for her.

She paused at the river's edge. Music so beautiful and tender that it took Brae's breath away flowed from the flowers, the trees, and even the rocks. Belita danced beside the river—swaying with the gentle rhythm of the music, turning graceful pirouettes. She laughed and waved at Brae.

He waved back, moving faster toward the shore. Then he was swimming, fighting the current that threatened to pull him back to the boat, back to his journey. The crowd was shouting now, encouraging, "You can make it!"

Brae went under and then surfaced spluttering and choking. He stared hard at the far shore. *I can see my parents!* Brae gasped, fighting harder. *Father! Mother!* Their voices joined the others: "Come on, Brae!"

The current grew stronger as Brae neared the shore. Jagged rocks jutted up from the riverbed, barely visible above the water's surface. One came out from the crowd and stretched out his hands. The folds of his robe fell back, and his scars could clearly be seen.

"You are the Wounded One," Brae gasped as he came out of the water, his eyes fixed on the scars that crisscrossed the arms and hands that drew him onto the shores of the Other Kingdom.

Immon nodded, his face only inches from Brae's. His shoulder-length brown hair, parted in the middle, barely concealed the puncture wounds on his forehead. "I am the Wounded One who heals your wounds," He confirmed.

Brae looked down at the scars that he had tried so hard to conceal on his own body. The scars on his back from Meriquoi's whip, on his head and arms from the beating in the Port of Plenty, on his wrists from the ropes that had bound him in the Land of Lasciviousness. They were all familiar scars.

Now, for the first time, Brae could see the abrasions on his heart, as if a light shone from within and illuminated him from the inside out. He watched in wonder as the jagged wounds and gaping holes in his heart mended. Sorrow and shame, rejection and fear, guilt and regret, all of these, and other pains that Brae could not recognize, drained out of him, and the holes closed up, the rends were repaired. Final healing, full and complete, was his as he stood in the presence of the Wounded One who healed all his wounds and freed him from all his pain. Immon took his arm and led him along the path to the banquet hall beside the throne room, where a feast was laid and a banner proclaimed Welcome Home.

Then, as if a curtain had been drawn, the Crystal River was no more. The Other Kingdom could not be seen. The *Seeking* bobbed gently on the Sea of Life.

CHAPTER 33
Asama's Demise

"W ell, that did it," Lucacius smirked. "You lost the subject."

Asama looked up from his smoky seat in the middle clouds, his fiery eyes smoldering.

Lucacius grinned, glad he was no longer afraid of the dragon. In fact, today seemed like a good time for a contest. "Do you think that I am ignorant that you hope to displace me?" the wolven taunted. "You may have been the big boy in Decarpia, but in middle clouds you are nothing."

Asama leapt to his feet, teeth gnashing, wings whirling. Rage roiled around him spreading like ink expelled by an angry octopus in the watery deep. He lunged at Lucacius, his neck extended, his beak gashing the wind.

When the inky darkness dissipated, Asama lay on his back, one wing shredded, the other twisted beneath his battered body. Scattered around him, like corn ripped from a cob, were 360 teeth. His scarred face hung in slack folds, quivering with each ragged breath.

Lucacius stood panting over the barely conscious dragon, exulting in his moment of victory. He lifted his enormous paw. With one swipe he would sever Asama's scrawny neck.

Asama closed his eyes. "End the pain. Send me to the pit." His failures closed around him, suffocating him, taunting him. "Just do it!" he screeched.

Lucacius grinned and brought his paw down hard. Suddenly he was on his back, all four legs reaching for the stars, his backside aching. His eyes rolled back in his head, searching for his assailant.

"Fool!" Dagog thundered, giving his general another kick, this time in his exposed stomach.

"I wasn't going to... kill him," Lucacius lied. "I just wanted to teach him a lesson, Master."

Dagog looked away from the wolven. His red-eyed stare scorched Asama's battered face. "Get up, fool! Kneel to your master."

The wounded dragon flopped and rolled in vain. He could not get himself up. Finally, he collapsed back into the cloud, waiting for annihilation.

After a few moments Dagog began to laugh. "Have you forgotten, Asama, that you are a form-changer? Get rid of the wings, cloak yourself with invisibility, and prepare for your next assignment."

The bewildered dragon raised himself to a sitting position. Gone were the battered wings, the naked beak. He ran his hands over his form, now invisible. He had arms and legs and... "Oh, my Master!" he said, "I am shaped like a man."

Dagog nodded. "And you shall find *that man* in an island by the sea. You want to be general and so you shall be, over a legion like yourself who will occupy this creature and do with him as I command. I have… plans for him."

Asama bowed before his master, feigning gratitude. *A costly reprieve,* he thought. *General over a swarm of flies.* The words were bitter in his mouth. *Imprisoned in the flesh of man….* He rose to his feet and stumbled off through middle cloud, searching for a man who dwelt among the graves in the city by the sea.

CHAPTER 34

Into the Unknown

T he sun was setting over the Sea of Life as Mikhail turned the *Seeking* into the wind. He grieved as the tall sails billowed, sweeping the ship into the open sea. Cumulus clouds, like great pillows, spread across the horizon, weeping warm raindrops. They pattered softly against the weathered deck, soaking the weary captain, who stood in silence at the helm, a battle raging in his heart.

He knew the will of Immon, but he wanted to be left alone with his grief. He wanted to cross the Crystal River into the Other Kingdom and walk the golden paths with Brae. He wanted to go home.

The Messenger laid a gentle hand on Mikhail's arm. "The lost still wait," he reminded.

Tears began to flow down the good man's face. Mikhail closed his eyes. He was tired. He wanted to go to bed, to sleep, to pretend that today had never happened. He would wake up, and Brae would be standing on the deck, at the wheel, guiding the *Seeking* on yet another journey.

When he opened his eyes, he gasped at the scene before him. The heavy clouds had parted like a blanket that has been split down the middle and furled back. Brilliant sunshine streamed through the opening, bathing the ship in golden light. A rainbow burst through the clouds on each side of the stream of light, creating an archway through which the *Seeking* sailed. Its tall canvas sails glistened in the light like pearls against the emerald sea.

Mikhail understood that if he sailed through the rainbow-enshrouded archway and basked in the warm glow of cleansing light, then he could not—would not—turn back.

Suddenly, Mikhail knew—though he could not say how—that those who cross over the Crystal River to attain the Other Kingdom are only a breath away from those who journey still on the Sea of Life.

So much thinking made Mikhail's head hurt, but his heart grew lighter with the hope ignited by such thoughts.

The Messenger laid a hand on Mikhail's arm. "There is a saying in the book," he said, holding up a thick volume that bore the name *Ancient Book of Mysteries*. "'Seeing that we are surrounded by so great a cloud of witnesses, let us run with patience the race that is set before us.'"

Mikhail knew of this book. Brae read it every day, near the end, and claimed that its pages were illuminated from within.

A sudden loneliness, so acute that it took Mikhail's breath away, swept over the grieving man. But the memory that wrenched his heart was not of Brea but of the beautiful woman that he had loved since his youth. His empty arms ached to hold her. *How can the death of one provoke such longing for another?* Mikhail could almost smell the perfume Anastasia had worn just for him, imported by their own ships from a land across the great sea. *If only she could sail with me now, on the* Seeking, *what an adventure that would be.*

Mikhail stroked his beard. *But perhaps she does. Perhaps she is as close as the clouds that swathe the sails.*

He rubbed his temple and shook his head, trying to clear his mind. *Where are all these thoughts coming from? They are too lofty for me. And yet, it is said that grief often tills the soil of the mind, making it more receptive to truths disdained before the suddenness of death.*

Mikhail's jaw set with new determination. He would sail into tomorrow with the Messenger at his side and dedicate his life to rescuing those caught in Dagog's deception.

"Immon, King of the Kingdom that rules my heart and my allegiance, if you send me I will go; I will pay any price, suffer any loss, to show the way to those who are willing to forsake the cities of their birth and enter upon the fair shores of the Other Kingdom."

But Mikhail was not to sail upon the sea. The Messenger pointed to the right, where a wild and desolate land was becoming visible through the mist.

"There," he said, "is where you shall go. You will not see me as you travel, but you must believe that I am with you. When the wind blows, know that I am in it. When the sun shines upon you, know that I am in the rays that warm you. When the rains fall, even then, I am there, cleansing the Kingdom of Adawm and replenishing the streams that give it life."

He offered Mikhail the *Ancient Book of Mysteries*. Mikhail hesitated. "Who am I to possess such riches?" he said. "This book has been treasured by others far more worthy than I."

"Take it, Mikhail," the Messenger placed the book in his hands. "This book belongs to all who would possess the Kingdom."

The embossed silver birch tree seemed to absorb the radiant prisms of the arc that stretched across the sky. Mikhail traced it with his finger; the tree felt warm to his touch. Courage coursed through him like strong medicine and he waited no longer. Dropping anchor in a small bay, he lowered the rowboat and rowed the short distance to shore. He waved to the Messenger, set his foot upon a path leading into a dense forest, and began his journey, one step at a time, into the unknown.

Letters to Lenore:
Diary of a Young Resister

Dear Lenore,

Today the Messenger left us. I know he said that he would be with us always, but I watched the Seeking raise her sails. I saw the glimmer of the sun upon the sea, split by the prow of the old ship, and the foaming swells that followed in her wake. I waved to the Messenger as he stood at the rail, waved goodbye to the one who sat beside me at our fires and wrapped his arms around me as I slept.

The drums have not ceased to sound since the Messenger set sail. Miammi and Miarrow whisper as they look toward Sodomon's tent. I have been told to gather my things, for tomorrow the Resisters will move deeper into the jungle.

Sadie refuses to go with us. "My place is here," she says with her jaw set. Who will teach me the art of words, Sadie, if you do not go with us?

Sodomon stalks through the village, stabbing at the ground with his palero—the stout stick that he uses on the heads of wild dogs that charge out of the jungle, and on the back of any person unfortunate enough to get in his way.

Miarrow calls. I must go. I will write more tomorrow when Machato awakens and chases away the chill of the night.

Love,
Salina

About the Author

Born in Newport, Arkansas, Linda Settles spent the first years of her life in a three-room house across the road from a cotton patch. The family had all the necessary commodities, an outhouse, chickens, and a dilapidated Ford. Linda was the oldest daughter, and her brother, Eddie (eleven months older than she), was her best friend and protector. When Eddie died at age nine, Linda suddenly became the eldest in a family that grew until there were six children, an absentee mother though not by choice, and a domineering father.

Linda always loved writing. As a teenager she wrote poetry that was often published in Latchstrings, a newspaper in North Little Rock. Having noticed her poems, the head of Poet's Roundtable of Arkansas offered her an honorary position in the Roundtable with a view to mentoring her, and invited her to their annual banquet to be introduced. Linda's father refused to let her attend, but she didn't give up writing. She wrote a poem about real estate that the Arkansas Democrat newspaper used to launch its real estate section. Linda was photographed and written up in the first edition.

Linda grew up and fled the Ozarks for Michigan, where she discovered how wonderful life is when one is free to enjoy it. She soon met and married Michael Settles. Linda and Mike are excited about the direction their life has taken and are thrilled to write each new chapter in the book of their personal Journey on the Sea of Life. There is much to be done before they reach the Other Kingdom, and they look forward to doing it.

Quest for the Other Kingdom series
About the Books

I began writing *The First Book of Journeys* ten years ago, when my children were young enough to sit on my lap and fall asleep to the sound of my voice. When I told the story to a classroom of children, they loved it, and people encouraged me to write a book about the characters and their journeys. But I was too busy home-schooling my children and working on my master's degree in counseling, so I kept telling stories and waited for life to slow down so I could write a book.

Originally, *Quest for the Other Kingdom* was a larger book, telling the story of three separate journeys. But as the characters developed and the work continued to grow, I decided to make each book a separate work that would stand alone and proclaim its own message to the world.

The First Book of Journeys is the story of a quest. It begins on the Sea of Life, and chronicles the adventures of Brae, an enslaved boy whose courage compels him to flee the City of Bondage and take his chances at sea in search of a better life. Lured by danger, and pursued by dragons, Brae finds joy and sorrow in his quest for the Other Kingdom. In the end, he discovers that nothing is ever as it appears in the beginning.

Diary of a Young Resister, the second book in the series, is a companion book to *The First Book of Journeys*. Salina, a young girl, records her journey in a hand-sewn journal given to her by her parents, Miarrow and Miammi. When faced with a choice between an easy life in the land of her birth, or joining the small band of Resisters who defy the claims of the Prince of the Darkness, Salina does not hesitate. Though she was only nine years old when she first met the Messenger, her allegiance to the great King Immon was secured long before the persecution of Resisters began. The ever-present threat of death cannot deter Salina from the quest, though her loyalty may cost her life.

The Second Book of Journeys, and the third, will follow the characters whose lives have been affected by the Messenger, the great King Immon, and the Emperor Addar through the pages of history. Their travels will dictate the number of journeys that comprise the *Quest for the Other Kingdom*.

I hope you come along and enjoy the journey.

~ Linda Settles

Edict House Publishing Group, LLC
Philosophy Statement

Remember the king's edict in the story of Esther? King Xerxes had signed a decree assuring the annihilation of the Jewish people. The decree could not be rescinded, though Xerxes regretted it, for he had sealed it with his royal signet ring. The Jews were saved by Mordecai's suggestion that they be allowed to arm themselves. Xerxes issued an edict granting the Jews in every city the rights to assemble and to protect themselves and their families.

We live in an era when the values that sustain the health of our nation and our lives are challenged on all sides. History records the age-old question "What is truth?" The answer requires a lifelong search. Every individual has the right and the responsibility to speak the truth as he or she perceives it, for absolute truth is our only defense against the destruction of our values and our lives.

We at Edict House Publishing Group, LLC are committed to publishing books that will facilitate the search for truth as they encourage, enlighten, and entertain our readers.